Claws

Claws

DAN GREENBURG

SCHOLASTIC INC.

New York Toronto London Auckland Sydney
Mexico City New Delhi Hong Kong Buenos Aires

ACKNOWLEDGMENT:
Thanks to Jennifer Arena,
whose skill at structuring stories is nothing short of dazzling.

ISBN-13: 978-0-545-04426-4
ISBN-10: 0-545-04426-X

12 11 10 9 8 7 6 5 4 3 2 1   7 8 9 10 11 12/0

Printed in the U.S.A.   40

First Scholastic printing, December 2007

For Judith and Zack,
who accompanied me on the big cat adventure

Claws

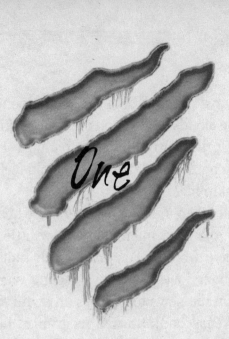

One

SAM HOUSTON TIGER RANCH.
TRESPASSERS WILL BE EATEN.

The driver of the rusty red pickup truck looked at the sign and moved a toothpick to the other side of his mouth.

"You sure this is the place you want, son?" he asked.

"This is the place," said Cody.

"Well, it's your funeral," said the driver, chuckling.

Cody grabbed his backpack and his suitcase and hopped out of the truck.

"Thanks for the lift," he called, but the truck was already chugging away.

Cody watched it disappear down County Road 2433, billowing clouds of dust and oily smoke. Inside the moving truck, the early-July heat hadn't seemed so bad. Standing on the road now, Cody could feel the sun baking his skin like a potato.

It had taken four hitches and three hours of driving through rolling farmland and tacky little Texas towns to get here from Dallas. The truck radio played sad songs about lonely cowboys feeling sorry for themselves. On the news today was an awful story—a tiger in Las Vegas had attacked its trainer. Leaped on his back and bit through his neck, killing him instantly.

If a trainer could be killed by a tiger who knew him well, how safe would it be for a fourteen-year-old kid like Cody to be working around tigers who didn't know him at all? Was this a bad omen? A sign he shouldn't work here?

Cody was tempted to hitch another ride and keep on going. Then he remembered what he'd been telling everyone since he left New York—*I'm not afraid of anything.* So he unlatched the heavy steel gate and let himself inside.

Behind the gate was a rutted sandy road bordered by dry scrubby bushes. On the left side of the road was a one-story ranch house made of white cinder block. Through large windows in the front of the house, Cody could just make out a turquoise swimming pool in the patio. *This might not be such a grim job after all,* he thought.

On the right side of the road were rows of animal pens. Massive orange tigers sprawled in the pens, panting in the heat, mouths open, tongues draped over lower jaws like wet wash on a line. They gazed at Cody with superior indifference. One of them yawned widely, wrinkling its nose, revealing flesh-tearing teeth and jaws large enough to swallow Cody's head.

Staring at it, Cody shuddered. He was pretty sure the woman on the phone said he wouldn't have any direct contact with the tigers; he'd only be cleaning their cages when they were safely locked down somewhere else. At least that's what he recalled. They certainly wouldn't expect him to go inside the cages when the tigers were there, would they? No, no, of course not.

It had been a stupid idea to take this job. Well, he'd done a lot of stupid things in his life. Hitchhiking his way across the country was one of them, but he didn't have much choice. He had to keep moving so *she* couldn't find him. He was willing to do whatever it took to keep out of her clutches.

A woman in a straw cowboy hat and a faded blue T-shirt with the sleeves torn off came out of the ranch house and trotted briskly in his direction. This was probably Sunny Carter, whom he'd spoken to on the phone. From the way she talked, she was either an owner or a manager of the ranch.

"Hi there!" she called out. "You Cody?"

"Right. You Sunny?"

She nodded. When she got close, she stuck out a hand for him to shake. It felt both tougher and drier than he expected.

"Like I said on the phone, hon, this job's just for July and August," said Sunny. "I got a tiger wrangler on medical leave till Labor Day. You on vacation from school?"

"Pretty much," said Cody. *Pretty much* permanent *vacation,* he thought.

"Well then, the job oughta suit you fine," said Sunny. "It pays minimum wage—I think I said that, too. How old are you, hon, sixteen?"

He nodded, though it wasn't true. Cody was fourteen, but since he was six feet tall and already shaving, people always thought he was older.

"I'm goin' to be honest with you, Cody," she said. "This here's a very tough job. If you take it, you'll be doin' things that aren't so pretty."

"Like . . . ?"

"Like cleanin' out animal pens. Shovelin' tiger and lion crap. The big cats here eat five thousand pounds of meat per week. Nearly all of it is dead cattle the local farmers give us. So twice a week you'll be tossin' parts of cattle carcasses into the pens. And a couple days later, you'll be haulin' 'em out of the pens after the cats have chewed most of the meat off. Tigers like their meat a little rotty, and dead animals don't smell too great after a couple of days, especially in this heat."

She paused for a reaction. When she didn't get one, she continued. "Hey, I might even teach you how to butcher a dead horse."

Again she waited for a reaction. Again she got none.

She squinted into the late-morning sun. There were crinkly lines around the corners of her eyes from squinting and her face was very tan. Too tan, Cody decided, but pretty good-looking, except for the nasty scar that ran from above her right eye clear down her cheek. Had she gotten that scar from a tiger?

"Are you willin' to do the kinds of things I just described?" she asked.

He nodded.

"Then say so," she said.

"What?"

"If you're willin' to do those things, please say so."

"Why?"

"Because I want to hear you say it out loud."

Good-looking or not, she might be a pain in the butt to work for.

"I'm willing to do those kinds of things," he said.

"Good." Sunny glanced at her watch. "It's almost noon. I'll go get Deke. He'll take you to the bunkhouse, help you get your gear squared away, and show you around."

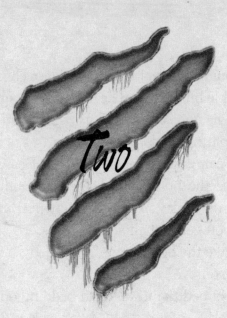

Two

"This here's where you'll bunk, Cody," said the old man.

He had a husky whiskey-and-cigarette voice with a strong West Texas accent. His name was Deke Halligan and he seemed to be another one of the bosses.

Deke was carrying Cody's bedding and towels. Cody carried his backpack and the cheap zippered suitcase he'd bought at a Walgreens in Chicago. They had walked down the wide sandy road from the main gate and the ranch house, past rows of tiger pens. They finally reached the bunkhouse at the other end of the road.

The bunkhouse wasn't much. Unfinished wood

walls, rough beamed ceiling, spiderwebs everywhere. Two double-bunk beds. The ones on the right looked occupied. The ones on the left were stripped to the badly stained mattresses.

"You can take either bunk," said Deke. "It was me, I'd choose the bottom one. We got another new man Sunny hired today, name of Dwayne. But you're here first, so you get first choice of bunks."

"I'll take the bottom one," said Cody.

"Smart move," said Deke.

He dropped the towels and bedding on the unmade lower bunk. Cody tossed his backpack and his zippered bag onto the bunk as well.

"You et lunch yet?" asked Deke.

"Nope," said Cody.

"Me neither," said Deke. "I'm so hungry I could eat a baby's butt through a park bench. Come back to the house and I'll cook us up some chicken-fried steak."

"Thanks."

Cody couldn't help staring at the eagle-globe-and-anchor of the U.S. Marine Corps tattooed on one huge biceps. The Marine motto, "Semper Fi," was on the other. Because of his white buzz cut and deeply creased face, Cody guessed he was around seventy, but he looked like he would easily win fights with much younger men.

"Okay, boy," he said. "Let's go get us some grub."

They walked out of the bunkhouse. The heat was

sizzling. It had to be at least a hundred degrees in the sun. Maybe more.

Since leaving New York, Cody had fled south and west, stopping in Pennsylvania, Ohio, Illinois, Kansas, and Oklahoma. It was lonely and scary to be only fourteen and entirely on your own. People expected you to know how to take care of yourself and how to act in unfamiliar situations. Like most New Yorkers, Cody thought he was street-smart and worldly, but he'd led a sheltered life and had learned few survival skills. When he left New York, he didn't know how to find a place to sleep or apply for a job or drive a car or avoid human predators. But he learned fast.

He'd had a long string of jobs—pumping gas, unloading trucks, waxing cars, washing dishes, delivering Chinese food. At a Dallas fast-food joint called Dusty's Tex-Mex, a boy named Mitch told him about the tiger-ranch job. Cody decided it had to be better than mopping restrooms and scrubbing toilets in Dusty's Tex-Mex. He quit and hitchhiked to the tiger ranch.

"So what do you think of Sunny?" Deke asked.

Did Deke really expect him to be honest about one of his bosses with the other?

"She seems okay," said Cody.

"Yeah," said Deke. "Sunny's tough as stewed skunk. But she knows more about tigers than a rabbit does about runnin'. You from back east?"

"Yep."

"New York's what I hear."

"Right," said Cody, hoping they wouldn't be going too far in this direction.

"We hired a fella from New York to be a tiger wrangler once," said Deke. "I thought you New Yorkers was supposed to be smart. This fella didn't know a widget from a whangdoodle. You got family back there in New York?"

"Not really," said Cody uncomfortably.

"Where are your parents?"

"Dead," said Cody.

Deke looked him over. "What year are you in school?"

"Oh, I don't go to school anymore," Cody answered, then remembered he told Sunny he was on vacation. Lying worked better with a good memory.

"You're a little young to be settin' off on your own, ain't you, son? A little wet behind the ears?"

"In New York State you can drive at sixteen and you can stop going to school," Cody answered. Making it sound like he was sixteen without actually lying.

Their walk toward the main house took them back past the rows of animal pens. Some of the tigers called out to Deke in yawning voices that sounded like Chewbacca from *Star Wars*. Deke stopped and talked to them. He got close to their cages and made noises that sounded a little like "Ff-ff-ff-ff-ff . . . ff-ff-ff-ff-ff," and a little like horses when they blow out through their nostrils.

"What are you doing?" Cody asked.

"It's called chuffing. That's how tigers talk to each other when they're being neighborly. Ff-ff-ff-ff-ff. Try it."

"Ff-ff-ff-ff-ff," said Cody, feeling stupid.

"Not too bad. Try it again, but this time add a little growl."

Cody tried it again. "Grrr-ff-ff-ff-ff-ff." It sounded more like what Deke did. The tiger he'd used it on looked at him with greater interest. It was as if Cody had suddenly spoken a Spanish phrase to a Latino.

"Now you know how to talk tiger," said Deke. "So how come you quit school, boy? You seem smart enough."

"My grades were lousy. But I'm just as smart as friends of mine who were getting A's."

"Come again?"

"I could've gotten A's if I'd tried," said Cody.

"Then why didn't you try?"

"It wasn't worth working that hard."

"Don't pee on my leg and tell me it's rainin'," said Deke. "If you got lousy grades and didn't do the work, you ain't so smart as you think you are."

They walked to the ranch house. Deke unlatched the gate to the front yard and they went inside. The clattering air conditioner made it about thirty degrees cooler. The living room was filled with oversized couches and stuffed chairs. The cushions on the chairs and couches were worn and soiled from years of being sat upon by rough men. The floors, once stained dark brown, were scuffed down to raw wood from being stamped on by heavy cowboy boots.

In the open kitchen were two stainless-steel sinks and a restaurant stove with twelve burners. Two industrial-sized refrigerators were layered with photographs of baby tigers and lions.

Deke cooked them chicken-fried steak, French fries, strong coffee, and peas out of a can. He didn't say anything till they were sitting at the table, eating.

"You drink coffee, son?" Deke asked.

"No, sir," said Cody.

"That's good."

"Good that I don't drink coffee?"

"Good that you called me *sir*. You smoke, son?"

"No, sir."

"That's good, too," said Deke. He took out a pack of cigarettes, lit one up, and sucked on it till the tip glowed orange. Deke's tanned skin looked like old shoes that had been dried too often on a hot radiator. There were yellow nicotine stains on the first and second fingers of his right hand. "Smokin' is a filthy habit and it'll kill you, sure as God made little green apples."

"Then why do *you* smoke?" Cody asked.

"Oh, it's too late for me, son. I already got cancer of the lungs." Deke erupted in a fit of coughing. "Yeah, I'm so sick I'd hafta get better to die."

Cody looked shocked. Deke slapped him on the back and burst out laughing.

"Naw, I'm fine," said Deke. "I was just pullin' your leg, boy. Well, I'm full as a tick, how 'bout you? You et enough?"

"Yes, thanks," said Cody.

"It's one o'clock. Let's us go out to the pens and start learnin' you the ropes."

Deke grabbed a few packages of frozen chicken out of the kitchen freezer and walked outside with Cody. A blast of hot air hit them in the face like an open oven. It had gotten hotter while they were inside having lunch. The heat made the air as wavy as a fun-house mirror.

Parked near the house was a Mule, a miniature red dump truck. The back of it had a deep bed that could be tilted up to dump its contents. The Mule was small enough to drive inside the animal pens to pick up poop and chewed-up carcasses before driving it to the carrion pits to dump its load. Cody hopped on board the Mule and Deke chugged to the pens. Surrounded by two sets of heavy chain-link fencing, each roofless pen was ten to twelve feet tall, twenty feet long, and twenty feet wide. There were many other similar pens on both sides, with walkways in between.

"You like these pens?" Deke asked. "I designed and built 'em myself. Learned from a fella who builds 'em for correctional facilities. Prisons."

"I know what correctional facilities are," said Cody.

"You'll notice I designed a small fenced-in section right near the door of each pen as a lockdown area. That's to keep the cats cooped up while we clean their pens. When you're shovelin' turds, the last thing you wanna be doin' is worryin' about gettin' your butt bit off."

In almost every pen there was an enclosed rectangular plywood structure not much larger than a tiger. It stood on stout wooden legs a few feet off the ground. One side had an opening just wide enough for a tiger to crawl in and out. The floor was covered with straw.

"What're the wooden boxes for?" Cody asked.

"Hidey-holes. Places for them to sneak away from the weather or their roommate. They like to drag a hunk of meat up there and gnaw on it without some other animal lookin' over their shoulder. But it's just one more thing for us to clean."

Cody wiped the sweat off his forehead with the back of his wrist.

"Hot enough for you, son?" Deke asked, chuckling.

Cody nodded.

"If I owned Hell and Texas, I'd rent out Texas and

live in Hell," said Deke. "You shoulda been here last week, boy. It was so hot I seen a dog chasin' a cat and they was both walkin'.." He looked around the grounds and shook his head. "If it don't rain soon, we're gonna have us some problems with brush fires."

"When does it cool off around here? October?"

"If you're lucky."

They stopped in front of one of the only pens that had a roof. Inside it were a leopard and something Cody figured was a black panther. They were both much smaller than the tigers and their tails looked a lot longer than their bodies.

"Most animals kill for food," said Deke. "Leopard is the only animal kills for sport—except for man, of course. I had to build me roofs on these here pens or the leopards woulda been outta here faster than a sneeze through a screen door."

"So tigers can't jump out of a roofless pen?" Cody asked.

Deke laughed.

"Oh, if they really wanted to, tigers could probably find a way to get outta these pens. So far they haven't wanted to bad enough."

"Which one's more dangerous, black panthers or leopards?"

"They're the exact same animal," said Deke. "In fact,

these two are sister and brother, Kamara and Kiko. If you look close at the coat of the black one, Kamara, you'll see she has spots, too."

Cody squinted at the black one's coat. It wasn't so much black as very dark brown. And he did see the spots. It looked like a child had taken a coloring-book drawing of a leopard and painted over it with dark brown watercolors.

The pen next to the leopards held two cougars. They were tawny. They were about the same size as the leopards and looked like small, slender lionesses.

"These here are cougars," said Deke. "Also known as mountain lions, pumas, panthers, and catamounts. Them and leopards are the only big cats that purr. You can either purr or roar, not both. Has somethin' to do with the bones in their skull—don't ask me what. We named these Oscar and Felix."

To the left of the cougars was a pen containing a young lion the size of a Great Dane.

"This here is Spanky," said Deke. "He's a six-month-old male. Wanna pay him a visit?"

"Sure," said Cody, knowing there was no other possible answer. Would it be safe in a pen with a lion, even a young one? Would Deke take him in there if it wasn't?

Deke let them into Spanky's pen, pushing the door inward and opening it just wide enough for him and Cody to squeeze through, then locking it behind them without looking. The instant they were inside, Spanky padded forward on oversized, floppy dust-mop paws and collapsed against Deke's legs, forcing him to sit down. Then Spanky climbed into Deke's lap and began rubbing his face all over Deke's, as friendly as a golden Lab pup.

"Hey, Spanky! Hey, buddy! How ya doin', good buddy?" said Deke, vigorously scrubbing the young lion's face with his knuckles. "Lions will love on you like this when they're young. They live together in big families in the wild, so they're real social. They're also real possessive. If you try to take away one of their toys, they'll protect it with their life. And if they bite you, they won't never let go."

Deke pushed Spanky off his lap and got to his feet.

"We leash-train most of the cats on this here ranch so's we can move 'em from one place to the other better. But lions are stubborn and lazy and don't see why they should have to walk on a leash. That's a real pain in the butt," he said. "What's even more a pain in the butt, this one has gone and quit eatin'."

"Why's that?" asked Cody.

Deke shrugged.

"Could be he's sick. Could be he's lonely. We had Spanky in with a young tiger about his age, name of Benny. Benny and him got along real good. Then Benny left."

"What do you mean, he left?" Cody asked.

"We was boardin' Benny for his owner, a wrestler fella by the name of Crusher. Big fella, wrestles for the WWF. You ever heard tell of Crusher?"

"No."

"Anyways, Crusher decided he needed Benny back," said Deke. "Now Spanky's all sad and stopped eatin'. You wanna pet him before we go?"

"Sure."

"Stick out your hand first so's he can smell it, see who you are, where you been, and who you know. Then, if he don't bite it, scratch him on the face like I done."

Cody cautiously stuck out his hand. Spanky sniffed it, then licked it with a hot, wet, coarse sandpaper tongue. Cody slowly moved his hand behind Spanky's ears and scratched. The young lion's fur was rougher than he expected. *I'm actually touching a lion,* he thought. *A young one, but still . . .*

Although Spanky was still frantic to be petted, Deke opened the door and he and Cody backed out of the pen.

"See you later, good buddy," said Deke.

They passed the pens of several grown tigers. The giant cats rubbed their bodies against the fence and made chuffing noises and languorous, yawning sounds. Deke showed Cody how to hold his hand absolutely flat against the chain links so the tigers could lick his palm through the fence with their gritty sandpaper tongues without chewing off his fingers.

They passed the pen of an enormous white tiger, a monster of a tiger. His heavy, muscular body looked to be ten feet long. He had thin brown stripes on a background of extremely thick white fur. A very broad pink nose with large nostrils. Wiry white whiskers, stiff as broom bristles. Ping-Pong-paddle-sized paws. Fangs as long as fingers. Claws designed to rip flesh.

"Who's this?" Cody asked.

"Name's Brutus," said Deke. "You don't want no part of this cat. He's meaner than a skilletful of rattlesnakes. That tiger shouldn't even be alive. C'mon."

They moved on and paused before a cage that held two grown white tigers. They must have weighed close to four hundred pounds, but they were only about half the size of Brutus.

"This here's Siegfried and Roy," said Deke. "Named for them fancy fellas in Vegas, had the white tigers in their magic act? There's only about two hundred white tigers in the world, so these are pretty valuable. Let me show you how we lock down the cats to clean their pens."

Deke walked over to the Mule and picked up a couple of packages of thawed chicken. As soon as Siegfried and Roy smelled the chicken, they loped over to the fence.

"This way, boys!" said Deke. He held up the packages of chicken and started toward the corner of the pen with the lockdown area.

He didn't have to coax them. The two tigers followed the chicken, their faces rubbing against the chain-link fencing. When they reached the small lockdown area, Deke lobbed the two packages of chicken over the top of the pen. The tigers caught the packages in their mouths and instantly tore them apart.

"I thought you fed them cattle parts," said Cody.

"We do," said Deke. "Twice a week. They'll eat anywheres from forty to fifty pounds of meat at a sittin', each of 'em, dependin' on the size of the cat. This here's just a bribe to get 'em into the lockdown area so we can clean their pen."

As soon as Siegfried and Roy were busy eating and growling, Deke stuck the handle of the rake through the chain-link fence and pushed the lockdown door shut. Cody noticed that Deke didn't check the locks very carefully. The tigers looked up and followed Deke and Cody with their eyes as they went on eating.

"A word of advice, son," said Deke. "Don't never interrupt a big cat while he's eatin', breedin', or fightin'."

Only the chain-link-fence door would now separate Cody and Deke from the hungry tigers. Was that enough to protect them? Deke had designed and built these pens himself. Of course they were safe. With the tigers locked down, Deke opened the vehicle gate to the unoccupied larger section of the pen and drove the Mule inside. Cody followed the Mule into the pen. *I am now standing inside a place where tigers live,* he thought.

Deke held out the rake. "You rake, I'll shovel," he said.

Deke put the shovel down like a dustpan next to a pile of tiger turds and Cody raked them into the shovel. It didn't smell nearly as bad as Cody thought it would. Deke dumped the crap into the bed of the Mule and they went on to the next pile.

Ahead of them was a grisly sight—a cow's rib cage with shreds of rotting meat still hanging from it and a cow's leg, from haunch to hoof, gnawed to the bone. Both were covered in a blanket of buzzing black flies. This was what was left of Siegfried and Roy's dinner from two days ago.

"Gimme a hand here, boy," said Deke.

Deke grabbed the rotting rib cage with his bare hands. Cody knew he couldn't refuse to help. He almost gagged, but he grabbed the slimy rib cage with both hands, and together they heaved it into the bed of the Mule. It was surprisingly heavy. Furious at being disturbed, the swarm of black flies buzzed loudly around their faces.

"Well," said Deke, "this here's one way to work up an appetite for dinner—eh, Cody?"

Three

By the time Cody got back to the bunkhouse, it was dark out. The end of his first day as a tiger wrangler.

Two of his new bunkmates were there, watching TV on a small black-and-white set with a wire coat hanger for an aerial. A couple of state-trooper patrol cars were chasing a white Mustang convertible through city streets at about a hundred miles an hour, ricocheting off parked vehicles.

"Hi, I'm Cody," said Cody, sticking out his hand.

"Randy," said a tall, blond cowboy with a tanned face. He wore boxer shorts and snakeskin boots and stood at an ironing board, pressing military creases into a pair of jeans. He looked to be sixteen or seventeen.

The guy sitting on one of the bottom bunks merely nodded to Cody and raised his hand in greeting.

"That there's Harlan," said Randy. "He don't talk much."

Harlan was older than Randy, maybe eighteen.

"Where you from, Cody?" Randy asked.

"Back east."

"*Where* back east?" said Randy.

"New York area."

"Manhattan?"

"Yeah," said Cody, getting uncomfortable. "You from around here?"

Randy nodded. "Saddler's Creek. You start today?"

"Yeah."

Randy reminded Cody of Charlie, one of the few boys he liked at Wellington, a private school for boys on New York's Upper East Side. Cody and Charlie loved to make fun of the headmaster's fake British accent. The headmaster was from New Jersey.

Before Cody ran away from home, he was in the ninth grade at Wellington. Five days a week he had to wear a blue blazer with the school's crest on the pocket, tan trousers, a white shirt, and a blue-and-red-striped tie. The only reason he went to Wellington was that *she* made him.

Despite what Deke said, if Cody tried, he could've gotten all A's. His mother would have loved that. She'd have bragged about it to all her stuck-up, phony friends. Every time he brought home a report card and she saw all his C's and D's, she was in actual pain. Cody got punished for bad grades, punished physically. It was worth it.

Cody went to the lower bunk he'd chosen earlier and sat down on it. His clothes were filthy and he could smell his own sweat. He opened his suitcase and rummaged through his stuff. He sorted through dirty socks, T-shirts, and underwear, careful not to let anyone catch sight of the moth-eaten old teddy bear with the crudely sewed-on head. He removed his black leather dopp kit and picked up one of the towels Deke had left him.

"Whatever made you want to work on a tiger ranch?" Randy asked.

"I don't know," Cody answered. "It seemed like a good idea at the time."

"What do you think of Sunny?"

"She's okay," said Cody.

"She strike you as a murderer?"

"Pardon me?"

"She strike you as somebody who could kill a man?" Randy asked.

"What do you mean?"

"He means folks around here think Sunny killed her brother," said Harlan in a low, growly voice.

"No kidding," said Cody. He wasn't sure if they were messing with him.

Harlan's acne-scarred face was creased into a frown. A cigarette stuck out of the corner of his mouth, the smoke curling right up into his eyes.

"Wayland disappeared four weeks ago," said Randy. "Nobody knows where he's at."

"So what makes them think he's dead?" Cody asked.

"He was supposed to be here for a weekly meetin' with our vet the following Thursday," said Randy. "He never showed, never called, and nobody's heard from him since. Wayland had lots of faults, but he's never yet missed a meetin' with the vet."

"What makes them think Sunny killed him?" Cody asked.

"Sunny and Wayland fight all the time," said Randy. "Loud, so you can hear. There isn't much those two agree on. The night Wayland disappeared was their worst ever. Folks here think Sunny cut him up and fed him to the cats. Buried his bones in the carrion pit where we throw the cattle carcasses."

Cody couldn't think of any answer to that.

"I'm going to shower now," he said.

Cody went into the bathroom—which was tiny, like the ones on airplanes—and took off his clothes and stepped into the shower. Hot showers always made him feel better. He tried not to think about what Randy and Harlan had said about Sunny killing her brother. He tried to think about the things he had learned today. How to shovel tiger poop. How to drag a rotting cow carcass out of a tiger pen.

He toweled dry and opened his dopp kit. He took out his electric razor and shaved, although his beard hadn't grown much since morning. He hoped Randy and Harlan would hear the shaver over the noise of the TV. Then he went back into the bunk room.

Randy and Harlan were still watching high-speed cop car chases, though Randy had finished ironing. Cody put on clean jeans and a fresh T-shirt. He lay back on his bed, his fingers laced behind his head, and tried to act interested in the TV.

The door opened and in came a big guy with shoulder-length brown hair, a scraggly beard, and six steel staples in his left ear.

"Hey, y'all," said the new guy.

"Hey," said Randy.

"Hey," said Cody.

Harlan nodded to the new guy and raised his hand in greeting.

"Name's Dwayne," said the new guy. He was so dirty it was hard to believe he'd ever been clean.

Dwayne shook hands with Randy and Harlan, then

came over to Cody. Cody stuck out his hand. Dwayne ignored it.

"You're in my bunk," said Dwayne.

"Well, no, this one's mine," said Cody.

"You're in my bunk, dude," Dwayne repeated. He leaned closer. He reeked of liquor.

"See, I was here earlier with Deke," said Cody. "Deke said I could have either bunk. I chose the bottom one."

Dwayne nodded. "Now choose the *top* one," he said.

Randy and Harlan had stopped watching TV. This was more interesting.

Dwayne was six foot four and weighed maybe ninety pounds more than Cody.

"Whatever you say," said Cody.

Cody got up, stripped the sheets off his mattress, and put them on the top bunk. Randy and Harlan went back to their cop car chases.

That night, about an hour after he fell asleep in his upper bunk, Cody slid into a confusing dream. He was wandering through some kind of circus sideshow and found himself right up against the stage.

Onstage, a man wearing a striped vest and a flat straw hat with a narrow brim was speaking into a microphone. The man's voice boomed off the walls.

"Ladies and gentlemen," said the man, "in back of

me are two doors. Behind one waits a dangerous white Siberian tiger. Behind the other door waits a beautiful lady, who holds a check for one million dollars! I dare anyone in this audience to come up here and tell me which door to open. Will it be the lady or the tiger? Instant riches or instant death? Who among you is brave enough to come up here and make that choice?"

The man leaned his microphone down to Cody.

"What about you, son? Are you scared to come up onstage and take a chance?"

"I'm not scared of anything," Cody heard himself saying.

"Did you hear that, ladies and gentlemen? This young man isn't scared of *anything*! Come on up here, son."

Cody walked up onstage.

"All right now, boy, the choice is yours," said the man. "Which do you choose—the door on the left or the door on the right?"

Cody looked at the two doors and the silk curtains that covered each of them. They were identical. From somewhere he heard a low growl. He couldn't tell which door it was coming from.

"Make your choice now, son," said the man. "Which door do you choose?"

Cody took a deep breath and pointed. "That one," he said.

The man stepped to the door on the left. He flung aside the silk curtain. He opened the door. The audience gasped. There in the doorway stood . . . a beautiful lady. It was Cody's mother.

But she had no check for a million dollars. And her fingernails suddenly turned into sharp claws. She sprang at Cody and began ripping at his flesh.

When he woke, Randy and Harlan were reaching up, trying to make him stop screaming.

"Hey, Cody!" said Randy. "You're havin' a nightmare!"

Dwayne got out of bed and stared up at him with sleepy anger.

"How many more times am I gonna be waked up by your screamin' and hollerin'?" Dwayne demanded.

"I'm not doing this because I *want* to," said Cody.

Four

When Cody was five years old, the love tests began.

"Teddy, how much do you love Mommy?" she asked.

"A whole bunch, Mommy," he said in his high toddler voice.

"Good. Do you love Mommy more than anybody in the world?"

He giggled.

"Mommy really wants to know this, sweetie," she said. "Do you love her more than anybody in the whole entire world?"

"Yes, Mommy."

"Good, Teddy. Do you love Mommy more than any of your toys?"

He thought it was a game.

"Yes, Mommy."

"Good, Teddy. Even more than your teddy bear?"

"Yes, Mommy."

"Good, Teddy. Would you still love Mommy if she took away your teddy bear?"

He giggled, not understanding.

Smiling, she grabbed his teddy bear.

"There. Mommy took your bear away, sweetie. Do you still love her?"

He nodded and reached out for his bear. She held it just beyond his reach.

"Would you still love Mommy if she hurt your bear?"

He was confused.

"Would you, sweetie? Mommy has to know. Would you still love her if she hurt your bear?"

"Yes, Mommy."

"Good."

She threw his teddy bear hard against the wall. His eyes widened in surprise.

"Do you still love Mommy, sweetie?" she asked.

He looked at his teddy bear, lying on the rug. He went to pick it up. She snatched it out of his grasp and held it once more out of reach.

"Do you still love Mommy, Teddy? Answer me."

"Yes, Mommy," he answered, somewhat uncertainly.

"Good," she said, smiling. "Very good, Teddy. Tell me. Would you still love Mommy if she cut off your teddy bear's head?"

"Are you going to cut off my teddy bear's head?" he asked, tears welling.

"No, no, of course not, sweetie. But would you still love Mommy if she did?"

"Please don't cut off my teddy bear's head," he whispered.

"I won't," she said. "I promise. But would you still love me if I did?"

He didn't answer.

"Would you or wouldn't you?" she asked.

He didn't answer.

She grabbed a pair of large sewing scissors, stuck the blades into the bear's neck, and snipped. The small head dropped to the floor.

He stared in shock at his favorite toy, now headless. Then he burst into hysterical tears.

She watched him carefully.

"Do you still love Mommy, sweetie?"

The day after the incident, she apologized and sewed the teddy bear's head back on with crude stitches. But he had learned a valuable lesson—how dangerous it was to have Mommy doubt his love. It also taught him another lesson—to always be on guard with her, to never again believe her promises.

If only he'd told her right away what she'd asked him—that he'd love her even if she cut off the bear's head—then maybe she wouldn't have done it. He blamed himself for what she'd done to his teddy. He began to think of himself as Cody, not as Teddy, the name that *she* had given him.

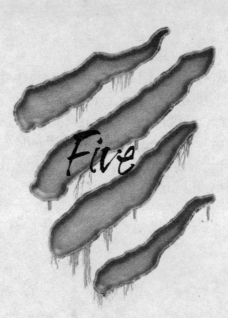

Randy, Harlan, and Dwayne all rolled out of bed the next morning at six o'clock sharp. Cody got to use the bathroom only after everybody else had finished. While Cody was brushing his teeth, Dwayne stuck his head back in.

"Hey, dude, you got a comb I can borrow?" Dwayne asked.

"A comb?" Cody couldn't believe the guy who'd forced him to switch beds and been so nasty about his nightmare was now asking him a favor.

"Yeah, a comb," said Dwayne. He was staring at Cody's comb on the sink.

"I don't think you'd want *this* comb," said Cody.

"Why not?"

"Well . . . I've got dandruff," said Cody, thinking fast.

"That's okay," said Dwayne. "So do I."

"Yeah, well, to tell you the truth," said Cody, "I'm really not too comfortable lending anybody my comb. It's a health thing."

"Uh-huh," said Dwayne. "Okay. You got a brush, then?"

Cody shook his head. "Nope. Just the comb."

There was an uncomfortable pause as Cody waited for an explosion.

"Okay," said Dwayne cheerfully. "No problem." He left the bathroom.

Cody shook his head and put the comb into his pocket.

He left the bunkhouse. The sun had just come up. It was pleasantly cool on the ranch this early, and a breeze carried something sweet on the air that smelled like honeysuckle. On the way to the main house for breakfast, Cody walked between long aisles of animal pens. The tigers watched him pass, thinking their tiger thoughts.

One of the pens he passed held Brutus, the giant white tiger. Cody stopped. Thirty feet away, at the back of the pen, the beast was studying him. Cody cautiously approached the chain-link fence.

"Hey, Brutus," Cody whispered. "How ya doin', boy?"

The great white tiger remained motionless. If he'd heard Cody, he gave no indication. Like many tigers on the ranch who were leash-trained, Brutus wore a thick leather collar. Cody wondered how long it had been since anybody had walked Brutus on a leash. Cody looked into his eyes. They weren't gold like other tigers' but ice-blue. The ice-blue eyes seemed to be considering which parts of Cody might be the tastiest.

Remembering Deke's lesson in chuffing, Cody leaned against the fence and began softly making the sounds tigers use to reassure one another: "Ff-ff-ff-ff-ff . . . ff-ff-ff-ff-ff." Brutus seemed intrigued by the noises, so Cody tried it again: "Ff-ff-ff-ff-ff . . . ff-ff-ff-ff-ff . . ."

Brutus was definitely listening. The tiger's ears swiveled. Cody could see the black-and-white bull's-eyes on the backs of them. *If I do this enough,* Cody thought, *maybe I can eventually get him to accept me.*

The tiger's ears flattened against his head. His lips pulled back from his teeth, wrinkling his nose.

Brutus sprang. He flew through the air, covering the thirty feet that separated him from Cody in a single bound. The impact of the eight-hundred-pound animal hitting the chain-link fence he was leaning on threw Cody backward into the dirt.

The tiger roared at Cody through the fence. Cody felt the vibrations of the roar throughout his body. The chain links that separated them looked way too thin to hold back something that ferocious. Cody remembered Deke saying tigers could get through a chain-link fence if they really wanted to.

Heart pumping in his throat, Cody scuttled sideways away from the fence without daring to stand.

Well, so much for getting him to accept me, Cody thought.

Breakfast was laid out, buffet-style, on the long table in the ranch house living room. Scrambled eggs, bacon, ham, sausages, flapjacks, fries, and grits. There was a huge thermos of coffee, a huge pitcher of orange juice, a carton of milk, and several little boxes of cereals. Froot Loops, Frosted Flakes, Trix, Cocoa Krispies, Count Chocula—cereals that seemed more for kids than for the rough Texas cowboys in the room.

Deke was standing at the far end of the room, eating and talking to Randy. Harlan was sitting down, eating alone. Dwayne was standing near the window, sipping a Coke and staring out into space. Sunny was pouring herself a cup of coffee in the kitchen.

Cody went over to the table and tried to figure out what, if anything, he wanted to eat. He was still pretty shaken up by the incident with the giant white tiger.

Sunny brought her coffee over to where Cody was standing.

"Mornin', Cody," she said.

"Morning."

"How are you gettin' along with your new room-mates?"

"Okay, I guess," he said.

Cody felt a little unsteady.

"Are you all right, hon?" she asked.

"Yeah, perfect."

"You sure?"

"Yeah, I'm perfect."

"Good," she said. "Deke tells me you've quit school."

"Uh, right."

"But you told me you were on vacation."

"True."

"So which is it?" she asked. "Did you quit school or are you on vacation?"

"Sort of both."

"How could it be both?"

"Well, I *am* on vacation, and I'm probably not going back in fall."

"Why aren't you goin' back in fall?" she asked.

He looked at her, trying to decide how to answer.

"Personal reasons."

"Want to tell me what they are?"

"Maybe sometime," he said.

"But not now?"

"But not now."

"Okay," she said. "You *are* sixteen, though? That part was true?"

He nodded.

"That means yes?" she asked. "I need the truth here, Cody."

"Uh-huh."

"You don't seem sure," she said. "Can I see a picture ID?"

He nodded dully. He fished his wallet out of his hip pocket. He took out his ID card and handed it to her. She studied it a moment, then handed it back without comment. The fake ID he'd bought before he left New York said he was sixteen.

"Deke says your parents are dead." Her voice was gentler now.

"Yeah."

"I'm sorry to hear that," she said. "What happened?"

"I'd . . . rather not get into it right now, if you don't mind."

"Are you in some kind of trouble?" she asked.

He laughed. He thought of what the men had said about Sunny killing her brother.

"Everybody's in *some* kind of trouble," he said.

She sipped her coffee, never taking her eyes off him.

"Who looks after you?" she asked softly.

"I look after myself," Cody answered.

"And who looked after you before you started lookin' after yourself?"

Cody was getting uncomfortable.

"Are you asking all these questions because you need to know for the job?"

She shook her head. "Not really," she said. "I was just tryin' to be neighborly."

"Then if you don't mind," he said, "I'd rather not talk about it right now."

"Suit yourself," she said. Sunny walked away.

Cody thought she seemed annoyed. He wished he could confide in her. But he just didn't know Sunny well enough to trust her.

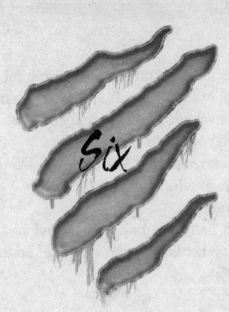

Six

Today was a feeding day.

Right after breakfast Deke showed Cody how to butcher a dead cow. How to cut off the legs and tail and head. How to slice open the belly and remove the slippery organs. Deke used a butcher knife with a wide blade so sharp it splintered bone. The butchering took about fifteen minutes. It was a messy, nasty job, and it probably would have sickened Cody even if he *hadn't* just eaten a big breakfast. Deke laughed his head off as Cody puked all over the sand.

When Cody finished vomiting and Deke finished laughing, Deke dragged the cow parts over to the front loader. The front loader was a muddy blue tractor with huge tires in back and small ones in front. A five-foot-wide steel bucket at the front of the machine could be raised ten feet into the air on retractable hydraulic arms. Deke piled cow parts into the bucket.

Cody stared at the bloody mess in the bucket.

"What you thinkin'?" Deke asked.

"Nothing."

"Don't lie to me, boy. You're thinkin', could Sunny have cut up her brother the way I cut up that cow, now ain't you?"

"Maybe."

Deke cackled with glee.

"Does Sunny butcher cows, the same as you?" Cody asked.

"Cows, bulls, horses, donkeys—whatever the neighbors bring us. Does it same as me, only better. Next to her, Jack the Ripper's all thumbs, and if that ain't a fact, I'm a possum."

Cody climbed aboard the front loader, and Deke drove him over to a row of pens. Whiskers and Jaws, the tigers in the nearest pen, who'd been lying down in the shade of a gnarled tree, immediately jumped up and padded over to the fence.

"All right, son," said Deke. "Now climb into the bucket."

Whiskers and Jaws made yawning noises, although they weren't yawning.

Cody approached the bucket. In it was a bloody mess. Cow legs and organs. He hesitated.

"Go on, son," said Deke. "None of that stuff's gonna bite you. It's all dead."

Cody gingerly climbed into the bucket with the gore.

"Good boy," said Deke. "All right now, up we go."

Deke threw the lever. The bucket, with Cody and the cow parts, creaked upward.

"Goin' up," Deke called. "Second floor, home furnishings . . . third floor, children's wear . . . fourth floor, ladies' lingerie . . ."

The bucket creaked to a stop at the top of the chain-link fence. Whiskers and Jaws licked their chops and growled with anticipation.

"Okay now," said Deke. "Toss any two parts over that fence into the pen there."

Cody shuddered at the thought of picking up the gory cow parts.

"C'mon, son. You already touched that stuff when it was dead two days and crawlin' with vermin. This should be a snap."

Cody picked up a leg and haunch and heaved it over the fence. It was heavy and it smeared his hands with blood. He thought he might puke again, but he held the retch back with his teeth. Both tigers attacked the cow haunch, growling, tearing, chewing, cracking the bones between their jaws.

"Good boy," said Deke. "Now give 'em somethin' else."

Cody heaved over another leg and haunch, because he couldn't bring himself to touch anything else in the bucket. The tigers leaped on that as well, continuing to growl with excitement.

Cody tried to picture Sunny standing by the chain-link fence at night, heaving body parts over the top. Parts of brother Wayland. The tigers scrambling on the ground. Was it possible? He honestly didn't know.

"Is it good for these guys to be eating all this stuff besides the meat?" Cody asked. "The hides and bones and stuff?"

"Why?" said Deke. "You thinkin' of trimmin' it away for 'em? Cleanin' it up and makin' cute little filet mignons out of it for 'em?"

"No, I'm just saying."

"Well, son, them parts you mentioned are actually real healthy for 'em," said Deke. "The hides are good for their teeth. They also clean out their system and give 'em their fiber. The bones give 'em their calcium. We feed 'em here the way they feed themselves in the wild—with no veggies or French fries on the side."

Deke drove the front loader to the next pen. Cody heaved more cow parts over the top of the fence to ravenous tigers. At the third pen he was forced to throw slimy cow organs. He couldn't imagine anything worse.

"We're about out of food here, Deke," said Cody. "What do we use to feed the others?"

"Don't worry, son. We got plenty of goodies back at the freezer. C'mon, I'll show you."

They drove up to a huge walk-in freezer. Deke lowered the bucket to the ground and Cody climbed out. Deke opened the heavy freezer door and motioned for Cody to follow him inside.

Clouds of condensation rolled out of the freezer into the hot Texas air as Cody walked inside. Because it was dark and because of the fog, it took Cody a moment to focus.

The first thing he saw was a severed horse's head—eyes staring, mouth open, horrid horsey teeth bared in a grimace of death. Just like when that rich Hollywood producer in *The Godfather* woke up and found the horse's head in bed with him. No, worse. Much worse, because it wasn't in a movie—it was right there in front of him.

The breath caught in Cody's throat. Everywhere he looked were stacked cattle parts—legs, haunches, tails, torsos, heads. A monster's toy box. The floor was slick with drying blood.

Cody staggered backward out of the freezer.

"Son," said Deke, "you look as surprised as a pup with his first porcupine."

Cody left the rest of his breakfast on the sand. Deke roared with laughter.

Seven

When he was five years old, she began reading him a bedtime story called *The Runaway Bunny.*

It was about a little bunny who told his mother he planned to run away from home. The mother bunny said if he ran away, she'd run after him. The little bunny said he'd become a fish and swim away from her. The mother bunny said if he became a fish, she'd become a fisherman and fish for him. The little bunny said he'd become a sailboat and sail away from her. The mother bunny said she'd become the wind and blow him where she wanted him to go. Wherever the little bunny said he'd run, the mother bunny said she'd follow him. Running away from her sounded hopeless and frightening.

"Teddy, do you know how much Mommy loves you?" she asked.

He shook his head.

"This much," she said.

She held her hands as far apart as they would go, bending her arms backward.

"Do you know how well Mommy knows you, sweetie?"

He shook his head.

"Mommy knows you so well she even knows what you're thinking. Did you know that?"

He shook his head.

"It's true, Teddy," she said. "Mommy can read your thoughts. Mommy knows everything you think. Mommy knows everything you do. And Mommy can see you even when you're not with her. So she can always take care of you. And she can always protect you. Isn't that wonderful?"

He nodded, but he didn't think it was wonderful. It filled him with dread.

"And because Mommy can read your thoughts and she can see you when you're not with her, sweetie, you can never run away from her. Isn't that wonderful?"

He nodded.

"You won't ever run away from Mommy, will you, sweetie?"

He shook his head from side to side.

"If you do, Teddy, Mommy will follow you. Mommy will track down her little bunny and bring him back where he belongs."

It was March of Cody's fourteenth year, a month after he finally had the guts to run away from home. Cody had been in Chicago for about a week, staying in a rickety rooming house on the South Side. Although it was almost spring, a thick shell of pitted black ice still covered the streets and sidewalks, and the wind howled like a living thing.

One night after work, there was a knock at the door of Cody's room. Cody's landlady said there was a call for him on the pay phone in the downstairs hallway. He had told nobody at work where he was staying. He went downstairs to the pay phone and picked up the receiver.

"Hello?" said Cody.

"Once there was a little bunny who wanted to run away," said the voice on the phone. "So he said to his mother, 'I am running away.' 'If you run away,' said his mother, 'I will run after you. For you are *my* little bunny.'"

Cody quietly hung up the phone. His hand was shaking so badly he had trouble fitting the receiver inside its cradle.

Eight

Cody was just about to transfer a juicy, hot slice of mushroom-and-pepperoni pizza onto his lunch plate when a face popped up in front of him in the dining room window. As suddenly as it appeared, it vanished. Cody was so startled he dropped his pizza on the floor.

"Did you see that?" asked Cody.

"See what?" said Randy.

"That face. It's gone now." Cody stooped to retrieve the slice. "A face was peeking in through the window. Then it disappeared."

"If it was a kid, it was Idiot Boy," said Randy.

"Who's Idiot Boy?"

"Oh, he's stayin' at the neighbor's ranch for the summer, I think," said Randy. "He's not right in the head."

"Really? What's wrong with him?"

Randy shook his head. "Don't know. He's always over here, snoopin' around, though. Tryin' to sneak peeks at the animals. At us. Won't talk. *Can't* talk. He really gives me the creeps, I swear."

"Well, isn't he trespassing or something?"

Randy took a huge bite of pizza. "*You* read the sign," he said through a mouthful of melted mozzarella. "Trespassers will be eaten. Maybe one of the cats'll eat him."

Sunny drifted over to the serving table and poured herself a glass of lemonade.

"Now, who is it the cats are goin' to be eatin'?" she asked.

"Idiot Boy," said Randy. "He's been peekin' in at us again."

She smiled. "Speakin' of bein' eaten, Cody, this is your third day here at the ranch. I think it's high time you met the cats."

"Haven't I already met them?" Cody asked, seeing where this was going.

"I meant *inside* the pens," said Sunny. "You know, shake paws with 'em and chew the fat awhile."

"Chew *whose* fat?" asked Randy, laughing.

Sunny looked at her watch. "It's about twelve-fifteen

now, Cody. Why don't you meet me over at Chomper, Chewy, Horace, and Boris's pen at four sharp."

"Four?" said Cody. "Four was when I promised Deke we'd take the Mule into Saddler's Creek to get the oil changed and the tires—"

"Four sharp, hon," Sunny interrupted. She took her lemonade and left.

Cody watched her walk away, a dark feeling of dread filling him up.

"You wouldn't be *scared* of meetin' the cats, now would ya, Cody?" asked Randy.

"I'm not scared of anything," Cody answered automatically.

It was four o'clock. Time to meet the cats.

Cody and Sunny stood outside one of the large outdoor pens. Inside the pen, lying on its grassy floor, were four of the handsomest and most frightening creatures Cody had ever seen. Black stripes on furry orange backgrounds. Tufted, round teddy bear ears with bull's-eyes on the back. Huge, heavy heads. Wiry white whiskers. Golden eyes that looked out at you from the depths of faraway jungles.

"When we go inside their pen, Cody, don't let these tigers think you're afraid of them," said Sunny. "Act like they're no big deal. Act like you've been handlin' tigers all your life."

"Okay," said Cody. He had no idea how to act like that, or how his acting could possibly fool a tiger. Dogs could smell your fear. Couldn't tigers?

"If a tiger challenges you," said Sunny, *"do not back away from him, and do not run.* If you back away, you're sayin' 'Bite me now, bite me hard.' If you run, you're dinner. Remember that, Cody. It could save your life."

"Okay," said Cody.

"When you're inside the pen," said Sunny, "start countin' the tigers. As long as you're in that pen, keep countin' those tigers. Make sure you see all four tigers at all times. Never let a tiger out of your sight. This is very important, Cody: Never turn your back on a tiger. If you turn your back on a tiger, he's goin' to think you're prey."

"Okay," said Cody. He wondered again why he'd taken this job. He wondered whether he was going to have the guts to walk inside with her.

"All right," said Sunny. "Now I'm goin' to teach you how to protect yourself when the tigers mess with you."

When the tigers mess with me? On the phone, Sunny had told him the tigers would always be locked down in a small section of their pens while he shoveled out their poop. He'd expected to eventually touch a tiger in some totally safe way, like when it was asleep or drugged with tranquilizers or something. Tigers messing with him was a new and unpleasant thought.

"How are they going to mess with me?" he asked.

"Oh, they'll test you to see what they can get away with," she said. "They'll see if they can dominate you. They'll push you with their big heads. They'll put their big paws on you. But you're not goin' to allow that, hon. If a tiger puts a paw on your leg and you don't stop him, he's goin' to put *two* paws on your leg. If you don't stop him then, next thing you'll do is get bit hard."

"And how do I stop a tiger from doing these things?" Cody asked.

"You yell 'No!' and you smack him hard on the nose."

"Uh-huh," said Cody. "And when I smack him hard on the nose, isn't he going to, you know, smack me back?"

"No, he'll back off. These four cats were all born here. They were all taken from their mothers and bottle-fed from the age of two weeks. They've all been hand-raised by me, personally. They've all been trained to back off when you yell 'No!' and smack 'em on the nose. They don't back off because smacking 'em on the nose hurts. They back off because they want to please us, and because bein' disciplined is real humiliatin' for them."

"What if the tiger doesn't back off when I smack him on the nose?" he asked.

"Okay. If he looks like he's about to attack you? Distract him. Make a lot of noise. Tigers are cowards, Cody.

If you make enough noise, you'll probably scare him away. Yell. Wave your arms. Bang against the sides of the pen. Grab somethin' to fight him off. A rake, a stick, a shovel. If you can't scare him away, roll yourself into a ball like an armadillo. Pull your knees up to your face. Clasp your hands behind your neck, with your arms protectin' your face. Tense your body, but don't struggle. Strugglin' only makes a cat bite harder." She looked at Cody to see what effect this had had on him.

He wondered if *Sunny* was messing with him. He showed her nothing. If there was one thing Cody wasn't going to do, it was let anybody think he was afraid. He switched off his feelings, as he had taught himself to do when things got painful at home.

"Okay, Cody," said Sunny with a crinkly smile. "Let's go meet the cats."

She unlocked the first gate.

"You'll notice," said Sunny, "that every one of these here pens is protected by two locked gates. So if an animal ever manages to get past the first gate, the second one is goin' to stop him."

Cody nodded. They were now inside the first gate.

"Four rules, Cody. Rule number one: Always enter a gate by pushin' *inward;* never open a gate *toward* you. That's so's an animal can't push his way out when you're comin' in. Rule number two: Never open a gate any wider than you need to get through it yourself. Rule number three: Never forget to lock the gate after you. Rule number four: Never enter a pen alone unless the animal is locked down in the lockdown area. Do you understand?"

Cody nodded. Compared to Sunny, Deke had been pretty careless about the locking and unlocking procedures.

"Please repeat what I just told you," said Sunny.

"What?"

"Please repeat the four rules I just told you," said Sunny.

Cody sighed. "Look, I heard what you said, okay?"

"I'm sure you did," said Sunny pleasantly. "But repeat 'em anyways."

"Why?"

"Because I asked you to," said Sunny.

"Because you asked me to," he repeated.

Her smile faded. Her voice took on a steely quality.

"And because those are four of the rules around here. If you don't follow the rules around here, you risk your life. You also risk the lives of the animals and the lives of the people you work with. If you want to risk your *own* life, that's your business. But I won't let you risk the lives of the animals or the people you work with. Now please repeat what I just told you."

Oh boy. She was a definite pain in the butt.

"Never open a gate toward me, never open a gate any wider than I need to get through it myself, never fail to lock the gate after me, never go into a pen with an animal alone," Cody repeated in a tired, singsong voice. "Okay?"

"Did I hear a little attitude there, Cody?" she asked.

"No." He was starting to dislike her.

"That's good," she said. "We get enough attitude around here from the animals. We don't need any from the humans."

One more gate separated him from the tigers. *I don't have to go through with this,* he thought. *It isn't too late to quit.* He could simply refuse to enter the second gate—let himself out of the first one and quit. Sunny would think he was a coward, but at least he'd be a *live* coward.

"I'm goin' to open the gate now," said Sunny. "I'm goin' into the pen first. Follow me fast and shut the gate behind you. As soon as you get inside, get your back up against the fence and start movin' away from the door."

They went inside the pen. Cody put his back up against the fence as he was told and moved away from the door. The four tigers still lay on the grass of the pen, but they were now watching Cody with great interest.

"Cody, meet Chewy, Chomper, Horace, and Boris,"

said Sunny. "They're eight months old and they each weigh around two hundred pounds. I've raised 'em from babies and they're comfortable with people, but they are also wild animals and extremely dangerous. Each and every one of them is real capable of killin' us if they choose to."

"Thank you for sharing that," said Cody, but it was only a whisper.

"The two of us are on the buddy system now," Sunny continued. "We'll each watch the other's back. We'll each warn the other if a cat looks like he's about to attack. Watch their body language—flattened ears, bared teeth. Once a cat has made up his mind, it usually takes three seconds to spring. That's plenty of time to get prepared. All right, they're probably goin' to come over now and get acquainted. Remember, don't show any fear. Act like you been doin' this all your natural-born life. In a few minutes they'll get bored with you and go away."

The four tigers didn't look at all bored with Cody. In fact, they seemed downright fascinated. Cody had never before looked at a tiger without a fence or bars to separate them. Now here he was in the same space as four of them.

The tigers got up and ambled over to sniff him and get acquainted. Getting sniffed by a really big dog was unnerving, Cody thought, but it was nothing compared to getting sniffed by a two-hundred-pound tiger. He thought of the news story about the trainer in Vegas.

"Talk to 'em, hon," said Sunny. "They're nervous meetin' you, and talkin' to 'em is reassuring."

They're *nervous?* he thought.

"Cody, the one nearest you is a female named Chomper. Talk to her."

"Good girl, Chomper," said Cody. "Good *girl.*"

Cody felt stupid calling her a good girl, but he couldn't think of anything else to say to her. Chomper sniffed between Cody's legs and pushed her nose against his crotch. He suddenly felt numb from the waist down.

"Don't let her do that, Cody," said Sunny. "She's messin' with you. Say, 'No, Chomper!' and give her a good hard smack on the nose."

"No, Chomper," Cody muttered, barely loud enough to hear.

"Louder, Cody!" Sunny called. "She can't hear you. And smack her hard on the nose!"

"No, Chomper," said Cody a little louder, and gave her the lightest possible tap on the nose.

Chomper rammed her head between Cody's legs. The tap on the nose he'd given her hadn't impressed her one bit, if she'd even noticed it. Cody was not at all happy about the tiger's head in his crotch. He was afraid she might take a bite out of him, but he was trying hard to act like he'd been doing this all his life.

"Louder and harder, Cody!" Sunny called.

"*No,* Chomper, *no!*" said Cody.

He took a deep breath and, trying not to think about what he was doing, gave her a fairly hard smack on the nose. He couldn't believe he had just smacked a two-hundred-pound tiger on the nose.

Chomper raised her head to look at him. Her head was a whole lot larger than his. Her eyes were golden and yards deep. Her mouth hung open. He could see her teeth. The ones in the corners were more than two inches long.

Chomper studied him thoughtfully. She seemed to be saying, *You know I could bite you in half if I wanted to.* Then she backed away. Maybe she was impressed by Cody's nose smack. Or maybe she was just bored.

It works! thought Cody giddily. *It actually works!*

The next tiger padded heavily up to Cody and butted him in the stomach with its huge head.

"That's Horace," said Sunny. "He's messin' with you. Tell him 'No!' and smack him on the nose."

"No, Horace!" said Cody, and, again without thinking too much about it, smacked the tiger on the nose.

Horace studied Cody with the same thoughtful expression as Chomper and then backed away.

Cody didn't have time to savor this triumph because

the third tiger lumbered up to him, bent down to sniff his left foot, then carefully placed one large paw behind Cody's ankle.

"That's Boris," said Sunny. "You definitely do *not* want that cat to be holdin' your foot. Tell him 'No!' and give him a good hard smack."

"No, Boris!" said Cody, and smacked him on the nose.

Boris backed off and was immediately replaced by the fourth tiger, who opened his mouth, turned his head, and gently closed his jaws around Cody's knee.

"No!" said Cody, and smacked him also.

The skin on Cody's scalp and back felt cold and prickly. Sweat was running down into his eyes.

"That was Chewy," said Sunny. "Good job, Cody. You passed the test, hon. These cats are all real impressed with you now."

When the tigers lay back down on the grass, Sunny crouched down behind Chomper and took the tiger's huge head in her hands. She slipped her fingers into Chomper's mouth, just behind the fangs.

"Come here, Cody," said Sunny. "Squat right down here next to me."

Counting tigers, Cody approached Sunny and Chomper. Then he squatted down beside them.

"You see these?" she said, pointing to Chomper's fangs. "These are the canine teeth. A grown tiger's canine teeth are around three inches long. These are about half that. If you stick your fingers behind the canine teeth, you control the cat's head. And if you control the cat's head, you control the cat, so she can't bite you. Here. Slip your fingers into her mouth, just behind her canine teeth."

"That's okay, I'm fine," said Cody.

"I'm controllin' her head," said Sunny. "It's perfectly safe."

"I know," said Cody, "but I'm fine."

"Cody?"

"What?"

"Do it."

Cody slipped his fingers into the tiger's mouth. It was a hot, wet, eerie feeling putting his fingers into a tiger's mouth. Cody didn't believe that anyone but Chomper was controlling her head.

"Okay," said Sunny. "How'd you like to go for a walk?"

"Sure." Cody was relieved. The tiger demonstration seemed to be over.

"Good," said Sunny.

She took a thick nylon dog leash out of her pocket. Cody had noticed that each of the four tigers wore an oversized dog collar. Sunny clipped one end of the leash to Chomper's collar and handed the other end to Cody.

The tiger demonstration wasn't over.

"With your back against the fence," said Sunny, "start movin' toward the door."

"What about Chomper?"

"Don't worry about Chomper," said Sunny. "She'll follow you."

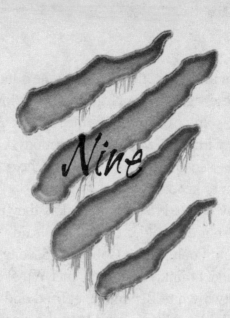

Nine

Once through the two locking gates and outside the pen, the tiger pulled hard on the leash. She was as excited as a big dog to be outside. It was all Cody could do to slow her down. A sandy path wound between the rows of pens. Beyond the pens was the bunkhouse. Beyond the bunkhouse Cody could see meadows of tall grass and hip-high weeds. *Look at me,* he thought. *I'm walking a tiger on a leash, just like I was walking a Saint Bernard.* It seemed unreal to him.

"Stay as far away from the pens as you can," said Sunny. "You don't want to get the other cats excited."

They passed between two rows of pens. Most of them housed two grown tigers each. Cody recognized

Whiskers and Jaws, the two tigers he'd fed the day before. These tigers were larger than the four Cody had just met, some two to three times as big. All the tigers watched with large yellow eyes as Cody, Chomper, and Sunny passed their pens. A few of them growled low warnings to keep away.

Sunny pointed to each animal as they passed.

"These are all older tigers," she said. "That there's Tigger and Pooh. That's Goliath and Kong. That's Rory and Claude. I think you already met Whiskers and Jaws, and the two white Bengals, Siegfried and Roy? In that pen are Jingles, Mittens, and Ivan the Terrible."

"How many animals do you have here?" Cody asked.

"Sixty-six. Five lions, two cougars, two leopards, and fifty-seven tigers. Most of these guys were born here. We raised 'em on baby bottles and formula. Some of 'em we rescued from abusive owners—circuses, zoos, or private owners."

"Private owners?" he repeated.

"Lotsa people in Texas think it's cool to keep tigers as pets. There's over three thousand tigers in Texas. That's almost as many as there are in the wild in India, Asia, and the whole rest of the world combined. Texans love dangerous pets. They buy a cute little tiger cub and they keep him in the house. He gets a little bigger and he rips all the stuffin' out of the couch, so they put him in the garage. Then one day he tears off somebody's arm and everybody's all surprised."

Her lips got thin.

"Tigers aren't pets," she said in a different voice. "Tigers are wild animals. They're killers."

"Then why do you keep them?"

"Because I love 'em," she said quietly. "When you take care of somethin' for a while, you start to love it."

Sunny's feeling about animals was somewhat different from his mother's. It wasn't just that Cody's mother didn't like animals, although she didn't. Partly it was that she had no use for things that couldn't do anything for her or her career. Partly it was that animals in the home, especially cute ones, took attention away from her. Cody's mother had to be the center of attention at all times.

When Cody was five, he found a stray gray tiger kitten whom he named Squeaky. Everybody loved Squeaky. "Look at that," said Cody's mother. "This kitten gets more attention around here than *I* do." Everybody laughed. The next day Squeaky mysteriously disappeared. Three days later Squeaky's tiny body was discovered behind a bush in the front yard.

Up ahead Cody heard the sound of roaring. It was a hollow, grunting, chilling jungle sound that echoed like it was coming over a loudspeaker. Chomper turned, jerked hard on her leash, and started off in the opposite direction.

"Don't let her go that way," said Sunny. "She's headin' towards the main gate."

Cody dug his heels into the sandy ground and hung on tight. Chomper pulled him along like a water-skier. Although he was only fourteen, Cody was strong. Chomper eventually stopped. She rolled over on her back and swiped at him with her enormous paws. Cody held the leash tight and tried to inch out of range of her claws, remembering not to back away from her.

"Chomper just got spooked by the roarin' is all," Sunny said. She bent down to scratch the tiger under the chin. "It's okay, darlin'. Don't worry, that bad boy can't get at you. He's all locked up."

"Who's doing all that roaring?" Cody asked.

"That's Brutus. A white Siberian, over eight hundred pounds. Biggest tiger I've ever seen. He hates everybody. And I mean he is *vicious.*"

Chomper got to her feet and started walking again. Cody followed, holding the leash tight with both hands. He decided not to mention that he and Brutus had already met.

"Why do you keep an animal as vicious as Brutus?" Cody asked.

"Well, I saw how bad he was bein' abused by this . . . *jerk* in West Texas who owned him, and I just couldn't stand it. So I bought him. Wayland thinks I'm nuts."

Cody decided to play dumb.

"Who's Wayland?" he said.

"My brother."

"Does he work here?"

Suddenly Sunny's eyes got watery and Cody thought she might be about to cry.

"Wayland's not here now, but you'll meet him," she said. "It's not really Brutus's fault he's the way he is. He just caught a couple bad breaks."

"What do you mean?"

"Well, his first owner was a guy who had a ranch near Amarillo. Brutus lived in a cage with another tiger, and they were buddies. One day they played too rough, and Brutus accidentally killed his buddy. He didn't know what he'd done, didn't understand why the other tiger had stopped movin'. Kept nudgin' him, kept tryin' to make him get up. When he realized the cat was dead, he got so upset he wouldn't leave the body, even to eat. Then he went into his cubbyhole and wouldn't come out for days. But his owner decided Brutus was a killer and sold him to the guy in West Texas. The West Texas jerk treated him so horrible . . ." She stopped and took a deep breath. "I won't even tell you what he did to him. Brutus became a real mean cat. Hates everybody now. Can't say I blame him."

"So what will you do with him, now that you saved him?" Cody asked.

Sunny shrugged. "Just keep him, I reckon."

"For how long?"

"For as long as he lives," she replied. "Indians say if you save somebody, you're responsible for him the rest of his life. In captivity tigers can live twenty, even thirty years. Brutus is around five, so I guess I'll have him maybe twenty-five years. By the way, you don't want to get anywhere *near* that tiger's cage. Except to clean it, of course."

The sun was very low in the sky by now. Cody sat on the grass outside the main house with Sunny. She took off her straw cowboy hat and ran her fingers through her nearly white blond hair.

They watched two tiger babies, Mary Jane and Sniffles, stumble out of the ranch house and waddle awkwardly toward them in the grass. The cubs were a little larger than grown house cats. They had fat chunky bodies, short thick legs, and oversized paws. Looking at them, Cody found it hard not to giggle. Their serious, fuzzy faces, their too-short whiskers, their high baby foreheads, their tiny, wide-set ears, their nearsighted blue eyes, made them a funny, unthreatening, miniature version of the dangerous adults.

They were so unbearably . . . *cute* that Cody was tempted to turn one over and look for a toy-maker's tag on its fat little belly. He picked up one of the wriggling tiger babies. Its stubby, muscular body was packed tight with tiny tiger parts. In the next eighteen months, it would explode into a fully formed, snarling six-hundred-pounder.

"Tiger babies need to be fed every four hours," said Sunny. "When they're two weeks old, we start 'em out on KMR—kitten milk replacement formula. From eight to sixteen weeks, we change the formula a little by adding raw turkey. Here, let me show you how we feed 'em."

She grabbed Mary Jane and cradled the cub in her arms. She plugged the nipple of a formula-filled baby bottle into her mouth. Mary Jane attacked the bottle like prey, sucking it dry in less than a minute. Sunny yanked the empty bottle out of the tiger baby's mouth.

"You got to pop the nipple out of her mouth before she starts suckin' air," said Sunny. "Then you got to burp her. Hold her tight like this, danglin' by one arm, and pat her on the back. It doesn't look so comfortable, but that's how Mama does it. You do it any other way, she's goin' to think a wild animal's got her."

Cody held Mary Jane the way Sunny had shown him, but he thought she looked uncomfortable, dangling by one arm. When it came time to burp Sniffles, he held her under both arms. The cub let out a sound like a human baby on a loudspeaker and bit him on the throat.

"Aww, isn't that cute?" Sunny cooed. "My little girl is learning how to kill."

As soon as both tiger babies had been fed and burped, they waddled back inside the house to curl up and go to sleep. Cody rubbed his throat where Sniffles had bitten it and checked his fingertips for blood, hoping Sunny wouldn't notice. There wasn't any.

"She's still got her milk teeth," Sunny explained. "Not sharp enough to puncture the skin."

Cody noticed a bunch of keys on the ground next to Sunny. They had probably slipped out of her pocket when she sat down on the grass. Attached to the key ring was a three-inch tiger claw mounted in a silver setting.

"What's that?" Cody asked, pointing.

Sunny picked it up and stroked the claw with a distant smile on her face.

"It's a claw from Sheba, our first tiger. Deke has one just like it. So does Wayland. We had these made up right after Sheba died. Good-luck charms." She put the key ring back in her pocket. "Hey, it's almost sunset. Let me show you what the lions here do every day, round about now."

They walked to the large lion pen near the front

gate. The lion pen had a hill at its center about fifteen feet high. At the top of the hill sat a 650-pound male lion with a dark shaggy mane so full it looked like he was wearing a sleeveless heavy fur jacket. He was keeping a careful watch over his kingdom. Near the base of the hill prowled two large lionesses.

"The guy on the hill is Caesar," said Sunny. "He's the boss of this pride. That thick mane he wears makes him look even bigger and more frightenin' to his enemies. It also shields him from lethal bites on the neck. Every day at sunset he and the gals start roarin'. They're announcin' that this is where the pride is goin' to be spendin' the night, warnin' strangers to stay away. Don't look at him now, hon, or you'll stop him from roarin'."

Sunny and Cody entered the perimeter fence and sat down on the grass near the inner chain-link fence of the lion pen. It was still pretty hot out, but not as bad as it had been earlier.

After a while, the sunset ritual began. First, one of the lionesses and then the other began a series of deep grunts. They sounded to Cody like sports fans in a stadium, grunting some kind of cheer.

The lionesses' grunting grew louder and faster until the grunts became roars. Then Caesar joined the chorus. Head thrust forward, Caesar's roars filled the lion pen, then the entire ranch, then the neighborhood for miles around. Cody could see the billows of vapor that Caesar exhaled with every roar. Louder and faster came the roars of the three lions, until the ground that Cody was sitting on began to vibrate and his whole body tingled.

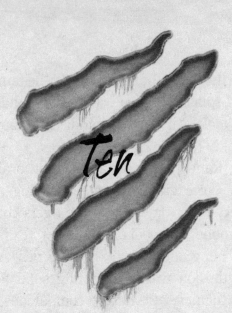

Ten

During the next three weeks, Cody got used to going into the walk-in freezer. Got used to handling cattle parts and feeding them to the animals. Got used to shoveling tiger and lion poop. Got used to dragging rotting carcasses out of the pens. Got used to hauling crap and carcasses off in the Mule and dumping them into the bus-sized carrion pits. Got used to using packages of raw chicken to lure tigers into lockdown.

Cody bottle-fed and burped the cubs, Mary Jane and Sniffles. In the short time he'd been there, he could see how much they'd grown and felt that he had helped. He took them into the pool, where Sunny showed him how to give them swimming lessons. Tigers are the only cats that love the water, but they have to be taught to swim. Panicked splashing gave way to dog-paddling as their instincts took over. As they paddled, he supported them so they didn't sink.

Cody, Randy, Dwayne, and Harlan drained and refilled the large galvanized-steel wading pools in the pens every other day so that the tigers could jump in, splash around, and cool off in the hot Texas weather.

Cody hung out a lot in Spanky's pen. Although the lonely little lion wasn't accepting solid food, he was hungrier than ever for human companionship. No matter how long Cody stayed in his pen, it was never enough for him. Spanky sat heavily in Cody's lap and licked his face with a rough tongue designed to rasp flesh off bones.

Spanky would suck on a baby bottle if Cody filled it with formula, but he couldn't be tempted to eat anything else. Cody tried feeding him chicken breasts. Spanky simply wasn't interested.

Sometimes Dwayne came into Spanky's pen to help shovel poop. Dwayne's breath usually stank from booze, even in the morning. He took great delight in sneaking up behind the young lion and roaring in his ear, or yanking hard on his tail like it was a bell rope, shouting, "Ding-dong, Spanky! Ding-dong!"

"Don't do that, Dwayne," Cody would say to him. "I

mean it. Spanky isn't well, and you're only making him worse."

"If he ain't well, dude," Dwayne would say, "then maybe we oughta put him outta his misery. Maybe that'd be the kindest thing we could do for him, don'tcha think?"

"Shut up, Dwayne," Cody would say, but it never stopped him.

Dwayne thought his routine was the funniest thing he'd ever heard, and every time he came into Spanky's pen, he did it again, complete with ding-dongs. Cody wanted to punch him.

Wild tigers prefer to hunt and live alone. Tigers raised in captivity can be taught to enjoy the company of humans and other animals, but only if taken from their mothers within the first two weeks of life, fed with baby bottles, given lots of love and attention, and trained not to bite or scratch. The tiger babies' biting and scratching was discouraged by saying "No!" and smacking them on the nose. Each tiger wrangler was assigned a young tiger and told to spend time every day in play and training. Cody was assigned to Chomper.

After a while, Chomper understood that Cody wouldn't allow biting or scratching, and she stopped testing him. Every morning and every evening he walked her around the ranch on a leash. Chomper loved to lie in the tall grass of the field near the gate. Cody ran his fingers over her broad forehead and her thick cheek fur and whisker pads. He scratched under her chin till she closed her eyes and raised her face in pleasure, like a house cat. If the bones in her skull had permitted, she'd have purred. He couldn't believe how quickly he'd gotten used to handling the younger lions and tigers.

Randy snapped pictures of Cody and Chomper with a disposable camera, but Cody had nobody to send them to.

One day right after breakfast, while taking Chomper on her morning stroll around the ranch, Cody spotted somebody lurking in the tall grass, spying on them. Idiot Boy?

He wondered what a kid who wasn't right in the head thought about people who walked tigers on leashes. If the kid was crazy, people walking tigers on leashes might not be one of the more unusual things he saw every day.

Cody put Chomper back in her pen and went to spend time with Spanky. The young lion still wasn't eating, but Cody continued brushing and currying him, talking to him gently, and making him feel loved. That's what he was doing when he spotted Idiot Boy crouching in the high weeds near Spanky's pen.

"Hey there," Cody called out. "Want to see a lion up close?"

Idiot Boy ducked down in the weeds and vanished from sight.

"You think I don't know you're there?" Cody called. "You've been following me around all morning. That's all right. I don't mind. I'd probably do the same thing if I were you."

There was a rustling in the weeds, but Idiot Boy chose not to show himself.

"Why don't you come out of hiding?" Cody called. "It's completely safe, you know. The lion and I are both in a cage. We couldn't hurt you if we wanted to. Which we don't, by the way. So show yourself. C'mon, what do you say?"

For a while there was no response. Then Cody saw a head pop up out of the weeds fairly close to Spanky's pen. The head was that of a boy about eight years old. He had a blond buzz cut and freckles.

"Hi there," said Cody. "Thanks for accepting my invitation. My name's Cody. What's yours?"

Idiot Boy just stared.

"The *lion's* name is *Spanky,*" said Cody, speaking slowly and carefully. "Do *you* have a name?"

"You d-d-don't n-n-need to t-t-talk to me like I was a d-d-darned *idiot,*" said the boy. "I ain't no d-d-darned idiot like they th-th-think." He had a strong West Texas accent. *I ain't no darned idiot like they think* sounded like *Ah ain't no durned idyut lock they thank.*

"Okay," said Cody. He was embarrassed by the boy's stuttering but pretended not to notice it. "What's your name?"

"Arthur P. C-C-C-Crawford," said the boy. "I'm here for the s-s-summer with my m-m-mama. I s-s-seen you walkin' that t-t-tiger on a leash."

"I know," said Cody. "That was Chomper."

"Ain't you s-s-scared that t-t-tiger would b-b-bite you?"

"Nah," said Cody. "Chomper wouldn't bite me. Chomper wouldn't bite *you,* either. Not if you followed the rules."

"What r-r-rules?"

"Well," said Cody, "first of all, you can't ever let a tiger think you're afraid of it. You've got to act like being with a tiger is no big deal. Like you've been doing it all your life."

Arthur nodded seriously.

"And w-w-what if he d-d-don't b-b-believe you?" he asked. "W-w-what if he . . . you know."

"What if he messes with you?" Cody asked.

Arthur nodded.

"You never back away," said Cody. "And you never, *ever* run. If you back away, you're saying, 'Bite me now, bite me hard.' If you run, you're dinner."

Arthur shuddered.

"I sure c-c-couldn't n-n-never get into n-n-no c-c-cage with n-n-no t-t-t-tiger."

"Well," said Cody, "maybe when you get to be my age, you'll feel different."

"H-h-how old are y-y-you?" Arthur asked.

"How old do you think?"

Arthur squinted at Cody.

"S-s-s-s-sixteen, I r-r-reckon."

"Good guess," said Cody.

This boy is no idiot, thought Cody, *just a very shy kid with a terrible stutter.*

After ten minutes of coaxing, Arthur got brave enough to come up to the chain-link fence and look at Spanky while Cody brushed the young lion and fed him from a bottle.

"I sure c-c-can't b-b-believe a l-l-*lion* would drink from a darned b-b-b-*baby* bottle," said Arthur.

"Right now," said Cody, "that's the only way he'll eat anything. He refuses to eat solid food, and that's a problem because when lions get to be this big, they're supposed to be eating practically nothing but meat."

"W-w-what's wr-wr-wrong with him?"

"We don't know."

After ten more minutes of coaxing, Cody got Arthur to put his palm flat against the chain-link fence. And when Spanky licked Arthur's hand, the boy smiled for the first time.

Eleven

The next Monday was Cody's third day off. On his first two he simply stayed at the ranch but got up late. This time, not knowing what else to do with a day off, he hitchhiked back to Dallas and went to see Mitch at Dusty's Tex-Mex.

It took five rides and three hours to get there. Cody hadn't thought to call ahead and see if Mitch was working. Mitch was sweeping the floor when Cody walked in.

"Hey, Mitch," said Cody.

"Hey, Cody," said Mitch. "What're *you* doing back here, man?"

"Well, it's my day off. I figured I'd drop by and say hello."

"Where you dropping by *from*?" Mitch asked.

"The Sam Houston Tiger Ranch."

"You're serious?" said Mitch. "You're actually working with tigers?"

"Yeah."

"Wow," said Mitch. "So what's it like, working with tigers?"

"It's cool," said Cody. "You know."

"Yeah."

Mitch took a quick look around. Then he whispered, "Hey, man, the *cops* been looking for you."

"What?" said Cody.

He was suddenly able to take only the shallowest of breaths. Something heavy as an elephant's foot seemed to be standing on his chest. He hadn't thought she'd check this far west. Hadn't thought she knew he'd gone beyond Chicago. Whatever made her check out Dallas?

"Yeah," said Mitch. "The day you left, a state trooper come by, asking about you. Saying you was wanted for something back east. Wanting to know did you work here."

"No kidding?" said Cody, feeling sick to his stomach. "What did you tell him?"

"That you didn't work here. That I never heard of you. I wasn't *about* to give you up, man. No *way.*"

"I appreciate that, Mitch," said Cody. "I mean it. Thank you."

"No problem, man. Hey, what do they want you for back east anyways?"

"Nothing important," said Cody.

"Felony or misdemeanor?" Mitch asked.

"Neither one."

If state troopers were looking for him in Dallas, Cody wondered, would they come as far as Saddler's Creek? As far as the tiger ranch? Should he leave the tiger ranch and push on to the next state? To New Mexico, as he had planned? To California or Oregon?

"Mitch!" called a voice from the back of the restaurant. "It's one o'clock. Are you working or are you on break?"

"Is it okay if I take my lunch break now, Dusty?" Mitch called.

"I reckon," said the voice. "Be back by two, though, Mitch. Sharp."

"Okay, Dusty."

They left the restaurant and walked out to the parking lot. Cody didn't want to push on to New Mexico or California or Oregon. He was just getting settled in at the tiger ranch. He was starting to feel at home there. But mainly, he was tired of running from her. He'd been on the run since February. Well, if Mitch hadn't told the state troopers about the tiger ranch, then they'd never look for him there. It was probably as safe a place to be as he could find right now.

"You want to get some lunch?" said Mitch.

"Sure. Where do you want to go?"

"What about the pizza place?"

"Sure," said Cody. "Whatever."

If you didn't stay in any place long, Cody thought, then you never had any friends. If you never had any friends, you spent your days off traveling three hours to have pizza with a guy like Mitch. Not that there was anything wrong with Mitch, but still . . .

They walked three doors down to the Doc Gomez Pizza Parlor and ordered a couple of slices and two Mountain Dews.

"So," said Mitch. "Tell me about the tiger ranch. How close do you have to get to them?"

"To the tigers?" said Cody. "Right up close. Right in their face."

"Honest?"

"Honest," said Cody. "We clean the crap out of their pens. We toss parts of butchered cows into their pens, and we haul out what's left two days later. We walk them on leashes."

Mitch burst out laughing.

"You had me right up till the part about walking them on leashes," he said, "I swear. What about the guys you work with? What are they like?"

"There's three guys in my bunkhouse," said Cody. "Randy, Harlan, and Dwayne. Randy wears snakeskin boots and gets his jeans starched. He's a good guy, though. Harlan frowns a lot and doesn't talk much. Then there's this guy named Dwayne. He's weird."

"In what way?"

Cody shrugged. "You can never figure what he's going to do next. Plus which, he teases the animals and drinks all the time. Then there's a good old boy named Deke. He's a real character. He's about seventy, but he's tougher than stewed skunk."

That was Deke's expression, Cody realized. Funny how Cody had picked it up.

"Deke is teaching me the ropes. He gives me a hard time, but I think he likes me. Anyway, he's my favorite. Then there's a woman named Sunny, who's another of the owners along with her brother. The brother disappeared three weeks before I got there, and there's talk that Sunny killed him. Cut him up and fed him to the tigers."

"No kidding?" said Mitch. "You think she did that?"

Cody shrugged. "Probably not," he said.

It took Cody nearly five hours to hitchhike back to the ranch. Getting rides after dark wasn't easy. He didn't get back till after midnight.

Twelve

Cody got permission to bring Arthur into Spanky's pen. For the lonely boy and the lonely little lion, it was instant friendship. Arthur spent hours brushing and combing Spanky, currying him with a wire brush, giving him massages. Spanky still wasn't interested in eating solid food. He was beginning to lose weight.

"He don't s-s-seem as s-s-s-spunky as he was b-b-before," Arthur observed.

"This little guy better start eating soon," said Sunny. "Lions Spanky's age can't survive too long on just formula."

Every couple of days, Deke or Sunny led a small group of visitors through the ranch. The visitors paid ten dollars each to look at and take pictures of tigers, lions, leopards, and cougars from the safe side of the chain-link fences, and another ten to get their pictures taken with a baby tiger. Cody helped whoever led the tours and was quick to pick up the routine.

One day Arthur joined the tour. When it was nearly over, a terrible commotion broke out in the vicinity of Brutus's pen. Loud roars and a man's shouts.

"W-w-what's g-g-g-g-goin' on over there?" Arthur asked.

Cody craned his neck to see. Hanging over the top of the fence of Brutus's pen was a man who looked like Dwayne. He seemed to be hurt. Brutus was batting at Dwayne with his enormous paws.

"One of the tigers is upset," said Cody.

Sunny tore off in the direction of the shouts and roars.

"Cody!" shouted Deke. "Take the tour back to the main house!"

"Right!" Cody yelled.

Deke ran off to help Sunny.

Cody turned to Arthur and the six adults who'd been on the tour.

"Okay, folks," said Cody, "that's our tour. We're going back to the main house and the gift shop now. You can buy souvenir T-shirts of the Sam Houston Tiger

Ranch and I can answer any questions you might have about the animals."

"W-w-what's g-g-goin' on over there?" asked Arthur again as Cody led the tour away.

People on the tour who had cameras and video recorders pointed them toward Brutus's pen.

"Nothing to worry about," said Cody, pushing Arthur back in the direction of the house. "C'mon, folks, nothing to see here. Let's just go back to the main house."

Leading Arthur and the adults back toward the house, Cody tried walking backward to see what was happening. Sunny and Deke had pulled Dwayne off the fence. Dwayne was now on the ground, swearing. Was he drunk? There was a pool of blood under his arm.

"What the Sam Hill were you doin' up there, you fool?" Deke was shouting at Dwayne.

"Is th-th-that guy b-b-b-b-*bleeding*?" asked Arthur excitedly.

"Did the tiger attack him?" asked a large woman in a too-small Dallas Cowboys T-shirt and shorts.

"I don't know," said Cody, "but everything's under control now."

"Is that g-g-guy g-g-gonna d-d-die?" asked Arthur.

"No," said Cody.

"H-h-how d-d-do you know he ain't gonna d-d-d-d-die?" Arthur asked.

"I just know," said Cody, looking back as he pushed people in the direction of the ranch house.

He could see that Sunny had whipped off her belt and wrapped it tightly around Dwayne's arm above the wound to stop the bleeding.

"How dumb do you have to be to tease a tiger like Brutus?" Cody could hear Deke shouting at Dwayne. "You're about as worthless as wet bread, boy!"

Now Deke and Sunny were dragging Dwayne toward Sunny's old pickup truck.

"Shouldn't they be taking that fella to a hospital?" asked a man in a Texas Rangers baseball cap, who continued taking pictures as Cody was moving him back.

"That's probably just exactly where they're taking him," said Cody.

"If these tigers are so dangerous," said another man, "why do you keep them here?"

"They're not dangerous if you're careful," said Cody. "That man was provoking the cat. It's not the animal's fault."

Deke and Sunny now had the door of the pickup truck open. Harlan and Randy had joined them and they were all pushing and pulling Dwayne into the truck.

An hour after the tour members left, Deke and Sunny were back.

"Well, we got Dwayne into Emergency at the

Saddler's Creek Community Hospital," said Sunny. "Then I fired him. Can you believe that drunken fool was teasin' Brutus with packages of chicken?"

"That boy's so dumb he'd hold a fish underwater to drown it," said Deke.

"How's his arm?" Cody asked.

"I'd say he has a fifty-fifty chance of keepin' it," said Sunny. "Which is about fifty percent more than he deserves."

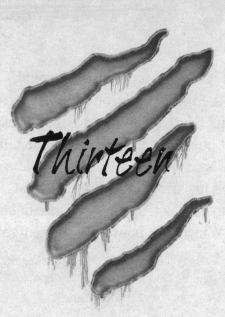

Thirteen

The very next day, right after breakfast, two plain-clothes detectives arrived from Dallas. At first Cody thought it had something to do with what happened to Dwayne.

"I have reported my brother Wayland's disappearance to the Dallas Police Department," Sunny told the staff in the parking lot next to the main house. "These gentlemen will be meetin' with each of you individually to find out if you know anythin' to help them with their investigation. I hope you'll give them your complete cooperation."

Cody didn't like the idea of talking to cops of any

kind. He was afraid they might recognize him. It didn't seem he had much choice, though. A detective named Runyon took him into the dining room of the main house for a little chat.

"What's your name, son?" asked Runyon.

"Cody."

"You got a last name, Cody?" asked Runyon.

"Foster."

Okay, so now they knew one of the names he'd been using. He also had ID cards proving he was Cody Pepper, Teddy Foster, and Teddy Black. It didn't mean they'd ever heard of him. And it would be downright paranoid to think that *she* would ever find out they had talked to him.

"What was the nature of your relationship with Wayland Carter?" asked Runyon.

"We didn't have a relationship, sir," said Cody. "He disappeared six weeks ago, and I've only worked here three. I never even met him."

Runyon made notes in a small spiral-bound notebook with lined pages. He took out a package of peanut M&M's and offered some to Cody.

"No thanks," said Cody.

Runyon shook out half a dozen in his hand and then began popping them into his mouth. Were these detectives beginning a homicide investigation and was Cody being interviewed as a possible suspect? Cody got a prickly feeling on the skin of his back and forehead.

"The night Wayland Carter disappeared," said Runyon, "Sunny Carter was allegedly heard fighting with him. Have you heard anything about that, Cody?"

"No, sir. That would have been three weeks before I got here."

"And where were you three weeks before you got here?" Runyon asked.

Cody had to think. "Kansas City, sir. I was working at a Chinese take-out place called the Golden Dragon."

"Where were you before Kansas City, Cody?"

"Before Kansas City?" said Cody. "Various places, sir. I'm making my way across the country."

"Where are you from originally, son?" Runyon asked.

"Originally, sir?" Cody dreaded the direction this was going. "Originally from back east, sir."

"Back east where?" Runyon asked.

"New York, sir."

"New York City?"

"Yes, sir."

"Do you have an address in New York City, Cody?" Runyon asked.

"Not anymore, sir. As I say, I'm working my way across the country."

Runyon regarded him thoughtfully and made more notes in his little spiral-bound notebook. Continuing to stare at Cody, he shook out more peanut M&M's and popped them into his mouth.

"What made you come to work on a tiger ranch?" Runyon asked.

"I was getting tired of mopping floors and cleaning toilets, sir. I thought this might be a nice change."

"Aren't you afraid of the tigers?" Runyon asked.

"No, sir."

"It's *normal* to be afraid of tigers," said Runyon.

"Well, sir, then I guess I'm not normal," said Cody, smiling.

"All right, Cody," said Runyon. "That's all for now. I may want to talk to you later, though."

The detectives interviewed Sunny, Deke, Harlan, and Randy.

They'd brought a search warrant and started poking around the ranch. They went into the walk-in freezer and spent a lot of time sorting through parts of cows, horses, mules, and donkeys as billows of fog rolled out into the hot Texas sun. Then they used the chugging yellow backhoe to go digging in the carrion pit.

Sunny watched as the backhoe's bucket dumped mounds of dirt and rotting cattle parts out on the ground beside the pit. After a while, the stench of decaying meat in the hot sun became overwhelming.

"What do they think they'll find?" Cody asked Sunny.

"Parts of Wayland, I reckon," she said.

The backhoe unearthed a gray-and-white-checked shirt. The detectives put on thin white rubber gloves to examine it. When they shook it free of dirt, the shirt had a large patch of what looked like dried brown blood on the chest and left shoulder. Detective Runyon brought it over to Sunny.

"Would you be able to identify this shirt for us, ma'am?" said Runyon.

Sunny nodded. She looked shaken.

"It's Wayland's," she said quietly.

"Thank you, ma'am."

The other detective took out a clear plastic evidence bag and put the bloody shirt inside it. Then he took Sunny back to the house for a chat. Her shoulders sagged. She looked pretty upset.

"What happens now?" Cody asked Randy.

"Now they'll run the shirt through their lab and try to find out whose blood that is," said Randy, a serious student of TV cop shows.

"Do they think Sunny killed him?"

"Startin' to look that way," said Randy.

"Just because he disappeared and they found a bloody shirt? That's not enough to prove she killed him."

"Wait till they learn she's done time," said Randy quietly.

"What do you mean?"

"Wait till they learn Sunny's done time in prison for assault," Randy whispered.

After the cops drove off, Cody went looking for Sunny. He found her in the house, staring out the kitchen window. When he came closer, he saw she was crying.

"Sunny, are you all right?" Cody asked.

When she didn't answer, he came up behind her and put his hand on her shoulder. She turned and fell into his arms, sobbing. He held her awkwardly, uncomfortable but unwilling to remove her arms from around his neck. It had been a long time since he'd been hugged by anybody.

"They think I killed Wayland," said Sunny. "I could never, ever do a thing like that, Cody—never, *ever.*"

"I know that," said Cody, patting her back, not knowing what else to do.

"I love Wayland," she said, "no matter how bad he acts sometimes. Even if I didn't, I could never do a thing like that, never, *ever.*"

Her cheek was pressed against his chest, her head just below his chin. He inhaled the scent of her hair, of her skin, and her fragrance drifted up his nostrils and into his lungs and spread throughout his entire body. It was a wonderful, clean smell, a slightly soapy smell. Not at all like the stench of his mother's expensive, sickly sweet perfume.

"The men say you were in prison for assault," said Cody. As soon as he opened his mouth, he was sorry. It was the absolute worst thing to say to somebody you were trying to comfort, but he couldn't help it. He had to know.

Sunny withdrew her arms.

"When I was workin' in the circus," she said, gazing out the kitchen window, "somebody was trainin' tigers in a very mean way. I tried to stop him. But he wouldn't stop. So . . . I pounded the crap out of him." She snorted at the memory. The laugh surprised Cody. "Assault in Texas is a Class A misdemeanor. They gave me a year in the Harris County Jail. It was . . . not a good experience."

Cody didn't know what to say, so he said nothing. Sunny started crying again. Cody liked that he was bigger and taller than Sunny. He liked the way her head had tucked right under his chin when she was hugging him. Cody felt he could protect her. He felt he *wanted* to protect her.

"I'll help you, Sunny," said Cody hoarsely. "I'll help you prove you had nothing to do with Wayland's death."

She looked back at him. She kissed him softly on the right cheek in gratitude.

He held his breath until she walked out of the room.

*   *   *

That night around midnight, after Cody, Randy, and Harlan had hit the sack, there came an ominous sound overhead. Faint at first, and then increasingly louder. *Thup-thup-thup-thup-thup, thup-thup-thup-thup-thup.*

Randy stuck his head out the door and looked upward.

"What is it?" asked Cody.

"Chopper," said Randy. "Cop chopper."

The police helicopter flew low and slow over the ranch, searchlights slicing the darkness, playing over the animal pens, the main house, the bunkhouse, the carrion pits.

The animals were awake now and frightened. They began to growl and roar. The growling and roaring were drowned out by the sound of the chopper.

"Why are they doing this?" Cody asked.

"To harass us."

"Why would they want to harass us?"

"I don't know," said Randy.

Cody went back to bed. He touched his right cheek where Sunny had kissed him. Before the chopper arrived, he'd been trying to remember every beat of the scene in the kitchen. Standing there with Sunny, trying to comfort her. Sunny sobbing, her arms around him. Sometimes he remembered it exactly the way it happened, with her giving him the single kiss on his right cheek in gratitude for his offer to help. Sometimes he remembered it with her kissing him more than once on the lips.

The following day the detectives were back. The blood on Wayland's shirt found in the carrion pit had been analyzed and compared with records at Wayland's doctor's office. The blood type matched Wayland's. It would take quite a bit longer to do DNA testing.

The detectives took Sunny, Deke, Cody, Harlan, and Randy into the main house, one by one, to question them again.

While they questioned Sunny, Cody waited outside with Deke.

"How did you ever get to be partners with Sunny and Wayland?" Cody asked.

Deke took out a cigar, bit off the tip, and lit it by striking a wooden kitchen match on his jeans.

"I knowed them from the circus," said Deke. "I was what they used to call a roustabout. Helped put up the tents, helped take 'em down, that sort of thing. Sunny was a trapeze artist and Wayland was a tiger trainer. Oh, he was never what you might call an animal lover, but he was a good trainer. Sunny's got a heart as big as all Hell and half of Texas, and she's got a whole entire different view on animals from Wayland. She fell in love with the big cats. When their daddy left them the land this ranch is on, brother Wayland wanted to ranch cattle. Sunny wanted to ranch tigers. Sunny, bein' the more headstrong of the two, won out. I lent 'em some cash. I also designed and built 'em the pens you see here with my own money, in exchange for bein' a full partner."

Deke chuckled.

"Wayland is somebody who spends the money when he has it, and sometimes when he don't. Sunny's a bit, well . . ."

"Thrifty?" Cody suggested.

"*Thrifty* wasn't quite the word I was lookin' for," Deke answered, chuckling again. "Sunny is *way* more than thrifty. Sunny would skin a flea for its hide. These big cats here consume five thousand pounds of meat per week. Most of that comes from dead cattle the neighborhood farmers give us, but it still costs us fifteen thousand bucks a month to maintain the animals. So Sunny's always watchin' the purse strings."

"Where do you get the money to run this place?" Cody asked.

"From contributions, from tours, and from people posin' for photos with the tiger babies."

"Is that enough?"

"It ain't doodly-squat," said Deke. "It ain't worth a pitcher of warm spit. It don't *near* cover our expenses."

"Was that what the big fight was about the night Wayland disappeared?"

"Yessir," said Deke. "A big entertainment corporation,

name of ValCom, offered to buy us out. We stood to earn us all a tidy profit. A very tidy profit indeed. Sunny hated the idea, God bless her, and said no. I was kind of neutral myself, but Sunny and Wayland was at each other's throats like junkyard dogs."

"I heard Sunny did some time in prison for assault," said Cody.

"Oh, you heard that one, did you?" said Deke, chuckling.

"Uh-huh."

"Well, did you also hear that the individual she assaulted was her brother Wayland?"

"What?" said Cody.

"Hey, boy, you sure didn't hear that one from *me*," said Deke.

When the detectives finished questioning Sunny, they drove away. Deke went in to talk to her. When he came out of the house, Cody stopped him.

"How is she?" Cody asked.

"They put her under house arrest," said Deke. "She can't leave the ranch without written permission from the cops. She looks like she's been rode hard and put away wet."

"Is there anything I can do for her?" Cody asked.

Deke shook his head.

"I'm hirin' her a good defense lawyer I know. Fella in

Dallas by the name of Clive Butterworth. He'll know just how to handle this."

"They haven't charged her with anything yet, though?" said Cody.

"No," said Deke. "Not yet."

Cody didn't want to believe that Sunny was a murderer, but it was starting to look bad. If she'd already gone to prison for attacking Wayland, wasn't she also capable of killing him?

"These are tough times, son," said Deke. "I ain't gonna blow smoke in your ear. Sunny is in this thing up to her ears. But Clive Butterworth is gonna do his best for her, and he's a mighty fine lawyer."

When Deke left, Cody went into the main house to look for Sunny. At first he couldn't find her, although he called her name several times. She wasn't in the living room or the dining room or the family room or the kitchen. He didn't want to invade her privacy by looking in the bedrooms, but when he passed by her door, he saw her sitting on the bed.

"Sunny?" said Cody softly.

"Yeah?"

"Is there anything I can do for you?"

She shook her head. She looked pretty depressed.

"Okay," he said. "Okay, Sunny, see you later."

He left and went back to work.

He threw a shovel, a rake, and two packages of raw

chicken parts into a wheelbarrow and walked to the pens to continue shoveling crap. Randy was dragging part of a rotting cow carcass out of a pen and getting ready to load it into the Mule.

"Let me give you a hand with that," said Cody.

He left the wheelbarrow and helped lift the heavy, slimy carcass off the ground and into the bed of the mini-truck.

"Thanks," said Randy.

In the lockdown area two grown tigers, Tina and Tony, were growling and tearing apart two packages of thawed chicken parts. Tony was limping, apparently in pain.

"What's wrong with *him*?" Cody asked.

"When he was a cub, his owner thought he'd be a better pet without his claws."

"So?"

"So to remove a tiger's claws, you gotta cut the bone out of the toes, back to the first joint. When the cat weighs twelve pounds, that's no big deal. When the cat weighs *six hundred* pounds, it's too painful to walk on."

Cody looked at Tony and shook his head. Randy started up the Mule.

"So how's Sunny doin'?" Randy asked.

"Not too good," said Cody. "I wish there was something I could do for her."

"Like what?" said Randy.

"I don't know. Poke around, see what I can find."

"You don't think she killed him?"

"I don't think so, no," said Cody.

"Yeah, well, just don't dig up more snakes than you can kill," said Randy.

Fourteen

The first time Cody found his mother lying on her bathroom floor, eyes wide open and staring, curled up on the white tiles like a fiddlehead fern, was exactly two weeks before his ninth birthday.

When he saw her, he erupted into tears, certain she was dead. He got down on the floor with her, rocked her in his arms, and begged her to speak to him.

For the past two days they had argued bitterly about which boy in his class at the Wellington School they would take to dinner and the theater on Cody's birthday. Cody had already invited his best friend, Charlie, without asking her first. His mother insisted he uninvite Charlie and choose a boy named Tyler Harrison instead.

Tyler Harrison was rich and snobbish, and Cody hated him. Tyler's father was an executive at the TV station where Cody's mother had her TV show. For two days Cody's mom had tried to convince him to change his mind. She begged him, bribed him, raged at him, cried hysterically, and gave him the silent treatment. Nothing could convince Cody to do the unthinkable. Then he came home from school and found her on the bathroom floor.

He begged her to come back from the dead. He promised to do whatever she wished, even . . . yes, even invite Tyler Harrison instead of Charlie, if she would only come back to life. His mother moaned and sighed and made a miraculous recovery. He spent his birthday with the boy he hated.

From then on, anytime his mother couldn't simply force him to do what she wanted, they went through a now-familiar cycle: she begged, she bribed, she raged, she cried, she gave him the silent treatment, she curled up on the bathroom floor, and she got what she wanted.

Fifteen

The police helicopter came back several more nights
in the following weeks. It buzzed the ranch for the
longest time, poking through the darkness with its
searchlight, keeping everybody awake and on edge.
The animals were more agitated than before.

After the helicopter's third visit in five nights, Cody
woke up in the morning drained of energy. His back
ached and his eyes were gummy. He went back to the
bunkhouse at noon to pour cold water on his head and
try to wake up enough to enjoy his lunch. When he
opened his dopp kit, he found the note. It was lettered in
pencil on a stiff piece of paper that had been carefully
folded over four times. The note read:

MAYBE WAYLAND AINT DEAD.
ROLLING THUNDER TONIGHT.

Who could have left him such a note? Randy and Harlan had the easiest access to Cody's dopp kit. There were others who roamed the ranch while Cody was working in the pens—a couple of construction workers, the staff vet, an electrician—but he barely knew their names. Probably only Randy and Harlan would know which dopp kit was his.

Maybe Wayland aint dead. Rolling Thunder tonight.

Did the note writer really think Wayland was alive, or was this a stupid practical joke? And what did *Rolling Thunder tonight* mean? Was *Rolling Thunder* a dramatic event that was about to happen, or was it the name of a place?

At lunch in the main house, Sunny was very quiet and barely ate. Cody chatted with Randy, Deke, and Harlan in turn, hoping to catch some sign that one of them might have left him the note.

"What's Rolling Thunder?" Cody casually asked as Harlan heaped his plate with chicken-fried steak and grits.

"A rock group," said Harlan.

"What's Rolling Thunder?" Cody asked Deke as he lit up a cigarette.

"A motorcycle gang," said Deke.

"What's Rolling Thunder?" Cody asked as Randy helped himself to more French fries.

"A bar in Saddler's Creek," said Randy. "Why?"

"Just wondering," said Cody.

"You're not thinkin' of goin' there, are you?"

"Why?"

"Outside of the fact you're underage?" said Randy. "It's supposed to be a pretty rough place."

Randy took his coffee cup and went to get cream and sugar.

So Rolling Thunder was a rough bar in Saddler's Creek and he was supposed to go there tonight. But if it was Randy who sent him the note, why did he advise against going there? If it was Harlan, why did he say it was a rock group? And if it was Deke, why did he say it was a motorcycle gang? Did they deliberately say these things to make it seem they hadn't sent the note?

All afternoon as he worked, Cody thought about it. The rays of the hot sun seared through his clothes into his skin. The sweat dripped down his body as he used hoses to refill the white plastic water buckets in the pens of the leopards, the lions, the cougars, and the youngest tigers. He chuffed to them through the chain-link fencing and put his palms flat against the wire to be licked by their rough, warm tongues.

In the late afternoon he saw Sunny at the back of

the house, hauling garbage to the compost heap on the far side of the swimming pool.

"Sunny, is there a bar in Saddler's Creek called Rolling Thunder?" he asked.

"Why?"

Cody gave her the folded note. She unfolded it and stared at it.

"Do *you* think Wayland's alive?" she asked.

"I don't know."

"Why would Wayland fake his own death?"

Cody shrugged.

"The guys say you two were fighting the night he disappeared," said Cody.

She nodded.

"The guys say it was a real ugly fight."

"The guys aren't wrong," said Sunny.

"What were you fighting about?"

"We got a buyout offer. The company wanted to get rid of all our old, sick, and problem animals. Euthanize 'em. Put 'em down. Then train the young ones—teach 'em circus tricks—and invite the public in and charge a fortune to see 'em. You gotta understand, Cody, these animals are all my babies. Every lion and tiger on this ranch I either helped the mother give birth to and then personally bottle-fed it and hand-raised it, or else I saved it from an abusive owner. Do you honestly think

I'm goin' to stand there and let 'em put my babies to death? Over my dead and bleeding body! I told 'em what they could do with their offer."

"But Wayland wanted to sell the ranch?" said Cody.

"Wayland and Deke both put a powerful lot of pressure on me to sell. I said no way. I am currently in the process of makin' this ranch into a not-for-profit corporation."

"So what did Wayland do when you refused to sell?"

"He said some ugly things. He stalked out and didn't come back."

So *both* Wayland and Deke had put pressure on her to sell? But Deke had told him he was "kind of neutral myself."

"I was thinking," said Cody. "What if Wayland just wanted you out of the way? Not enough to kill you. Just, you know, out of the way."

"Just enough to send me back to prison?" she asked.

"I don't know. Maybe."

"I reckon that's possible," she answered.

"I might be going to that bar tonight," said Cody, trying to sound as though he went to bars quite a lot. "Can I borrow your pickup?"

"You'd do this to help me?" she asked.

He nodded.

"Why?"

He shrugged. "I don't know. I want to help you prove you didn't kill your brother."

She looked at him and then looked away.

"Yeah, you can borrow my pickup," she said finally. "Try not to wreck it. You know how to drive?"

"Yeah. Do you have a picture of Wayland? I want to see if anybody there recognizes him."

"Sure, but don't worry. They'll know Wayland at the Rolling Thunder," she said with a bitter laugh.

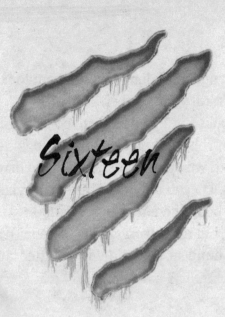

Sixteen

After dinner, Cody got the photo from Sunny. Then he went out to the parking lot and climbed into the rusted-out Chevy pickup truck. He saw dark stains on the seat and floor that must have been Dwayne's blood and tried not to have any feelings about them.

He spent five minutes sitting in the driver's seat with the engine off, moving the floor shift through the gears, getting familiar with it. By the time he finally started up the engine, he was able to pull out of the lot without making a fool of himself. He had driven cars before, even stick shifts, but not a truck like this one.

The trip to Saddler's Creek took twenty minutes. By the time he got there, he was driving the pickup as if he owned it. It took another ten minutes of cruising the streets in the town's tiny business section before he found the Rolling Thunder Saloon. He parked the truck and went to the window of the bar to look inside.

It was pretty dark in there. There were several hanging lights with lamp shades of green glass. There was a long bar with several bar stools. On the stools were maybe half a dozen men. They all seemed to be turned toward one guy, listening. The guy they were listening to looked familiar. And then Cody realized why.

The guy was Dwayne. And where his right arm used to be, there was now a stump.

Could it have been Dwayne who left him the note? Dwayne sure knew what his dopp kit looked like. Dwayne would never have been allowed back on the ranch, but he could have sneaked in while everyone was busy with the tigers.

Cody took a deep breath and walked into the bar.

Dwayne was telling the men at the bar a story. Judging by their reactions, it was a story they'd heard before.

"So there he is," said Dwayne, slurring his words. "Old Brutus. Most vicious tiger in captivity. Fifteen feet long if he's an inch. A man-eater they bought to pull the tourists in at twenty bucks a head. A thousand pounds if he's an ounce. So old Brutus is testin' me to see who's tougher. Tries to back me down, but I'm not buyin' it, see? Leaps on me and takes my arm off right at the elbow. I mean, there's my arm, lyin' on the ground. *Man!* I pick up the arm, I smack old Brutus in the face with it, and I go off to find the boss. 'Sunny,' I says. I says, 'I need you to drive me to the hospital, sweet thing, so they can sew this arm back on.' Only trouble is, by the time we get there, too much time has passed—the fool thing won't stick back on no more."

The men at the bar laughed politely or patted Dwayne on the back, then turned away.

Although he knew Dwayne had never really liked him, Cody took a deep breath and walked over to his bar stool.

"Hey, Dwayne," said Cody.

Dwayne looked up.

"Hey, kid."

"I thought maybe we could talk," said Cody.

"Go ahead," said Dwayne. "Talk."

Cody looked around.

"I thought we could find someplace a little more, you know . . . private."

"Okay," said Dwayne. "You want a beer?"

"No thanks."

Dwayne lurched off the bar stool and caught himself before he fell. He walked uncertainly to a small table in the back. It had a chair on each side of it. It had a candle in a red glass in the middle of it. There was red plastic netting around the red glass and the candle was lit.

"Sit down," said Dwayne, belching grandly. He made a comical bow.

Cody took a seat. Dwayne sat down very carefully, as if it were a delicate balancing act he'd been rehearsing for weeks.

He studied Cody for a moment, frowning with drunken seriousness.

"Hey, dude, how come you 'n' me never got to be buds?" he asked.

"I don't know," said Cody.

"Neither do I. I mean, we worked together, we bunked together, we shoveled tiger turds together, but we never got to be buds. It just never happened. You know why I think?"

"Why?"

"I think what it is, is we each of us got a whole entire different theory of tiger wranglin' from the other, is what it is."

"Okay," said Cody.

"See, I come from the theory of Tough Love, whereas you come from the theory of Let 'Em Do Whatever the Hell They Want. Y'see what I'm sayin'?"

"Uh-huh," said Cody, thinking, *The theory you actually come from is the theory of Get Drunk and Tease Them Till They Bite Your Arm Off.*

"You see this?" said Dwayne, pointing to his stump. "You know how this happened?"

"How?" said Cody.

"Old Brutus. Old Brutus testin' me to see who's tougher. Tried to back me down, but I wasn't buyin' it. Leaped on me and took my arm off right at the elbow. I mean, there's my arm, lyin' on the ground, right? I pick up the arm, I smack old Brutus in the face with it, and I go off to find the boss. 'Sunny,' I says—"

"I was told if I came here tonight, I might find out something about Wayland Carter," said Cody.

Dwayne nodded seriously, then leaned in close and whispered drunkenly: "What if I were to tell you Wayland Carter was seen alive in this here town as recent as last week?"

"You're serious?"

"If I'm lyin', I'm cryin'."

"Where was he seen?" Cody asked. "In this bar, you mean?"

Dwayne shook his head violently.

"No, sir. No, *sir.* No way, José. Not in this here *bar,* man. At a motel. At the Heartbreak Motel. You know it? The Heartbreak Motel? Named for that Elvis Presley song?"

"Can't say I do," said Cody.

"Since mah bay-buh left me," sang Dwayne in a

poor imitation of Elvis, "well, Ah found a new place to dwell. . . . Well, it's down at the e-end of Lonely Street at . . . Heartbreak Motel. . . ."

"I've heard the song," said Cody, cutting him short, "but I don't know the place. Where is it?"

"Well, it sure ain't on Lonely Street," said Dwayne with a huge laugh. "It's up on Mason, near the corner of Sycamore. Whyn't you go there, ask the desk clerk has he seen Wayland? See what he says. See what the man says about *that*."

"Okay," said Cody. "Maybe I will. Maybe I'll do that. Dwayne, tell me something."

"Shoot."

"Sunny fired you. How come you're willing to help prove she didn't kill her brother?"

Dwayne frowned and considered the question.

"Sunny also saved my life," he said.

When Cody pulled the pickup into the parking lot, he could see somebody sitting on the split-rail fence in the dark, waiting. Sunny.

"Did you find anything in town?" she asked.

"Not yet," said Cody, slamming the truck door. "But guess what? Dwayne told me Wayland was seen in town as recently as last week."

"Dwayne told you that?" she asked. "Dwayne, the

drunken fool who hassles huge white tigers? *That* Dwayne?"

Cody nodded.

"I went to the Heartbreak Motel, where he supposedly stayed last week," said Cody, "but the desk clerk is new and wasn't working then. I'm supposed to come back when the regular night man is back."

"Why is Dwayne being so nice after I fired his butt?"

"He says it's because you saved his life."

"Well, I'll be dipped," she said.

Seventeen

Even though he'd done it by himself twice before, cleaning Brutus's pen was not a job Cody was comfortable with. Just the act of showing the huge tiger the packages of raw chicken and then leading him along the chain-link fence into the lockdown area was terrifying, especially so soon after the tiger had reduced Dwayne's arm to a stump. None of the other tigers reacted to the lockdown process the way Brutus did, growling and snarling all the way.

When Brutus was crunching up chicken and the lockdown gate was securely fastened, Cody was still uneasy taking the wheelbarrow into the pen and raking tiger turds into his shovel.

The late-afternoon sun cooked Cody's skin through his T-shirt and his baseball cap. He had just bent down to pick up a slimy gnawed thighbone when he heard the slight creak of a metal gate. Leaning on his rake, he looked up and saw something he never expected to see.

The lockdown door had been pushed open. Brutus had padded quietly into the pen.

Cody stopped breathing.

The giant animal stared at Cody with ice-blue eyes, a low growl grumbling in his chest. His ears flattened against his head.

In his terror, everything in Cody's universe cranked down to slow motion.

Images pulsed before Cody's eyes:

Brutus flinging himself thirty feet across his pen the morning Cody tried to make friends with him.

Dwayne lying on the ground, a pool of purple blood spreading under his arm.

Dwayne's stump in the Rolling Thunder Saloon.

Snarling, the huge white tiger took a step in Cody's direction.

If a tiger challenges you, do not back away from him, and do not run.

Cody clutched his rake. Obeying his feelings and not Sunny's warnings, he backed away.

He couldn't help it. Backing away was an automatic

response. He knew what a horrible mistake he was making.

If you back away, you're sayin' "Bite me now, bite me hard." If you run, you're dinner. . . .

It was too late now. Cody had done the unthinkable. He had revealed his weakness and his fear, and now the animal would rip him apart.

Brutus reared up on his hind legs. Now several feet above Cody's head, the tiger was impossibly tall. His jaws opened wide. His lips pulled back to reveal curved yellow fangs over three inches long. His wide pink tongue glistened. Saliva dripped from his jaws.

Cody's heart beat so violently his body shook. His breath was strangled in his throat. He had never seen anything so frightening, so horrifyingly unreal.

He wondered when the attack would come. He wondered what it would feel like to be eaten alive by the biggest tiger in the world.

One horrible bite from those incredible jaws and it would all be over. Unimaginable, excruciating pain for an instant, and then a swamp of darkness would swallow him up and he would never know anything again.

No! He couldn't give up. He had to do something!

Brutus roared and the ground shuddered. Claws splayed wide, front legs outstretched like Frankenstein's monster, the tiger staggered toward Cody.

Distract him. Make a lot of noise. Tigers are cowards, Cody. If you make enough noise, you'll probably scare him away. . . .

Cody could not move. His legs had grown roots and planted themselves as firmly as tree trunks in the sandy soil of the pen. He was unable to activate a single muscle or tendon.

He wanted to cry. He wanted to scream for help. But there was nobody near to hear his screams, and no way for them to help him if they did.

Unless he did something, and did it immediately, he would be torn to pieces—reduced to the slick red body parts he'd thrown over the fence to the voracious tigers.

Yell. Wave your arms. Bang against the sides of the pen. Tigers are cowards, Cody. . . . Tigers are cowards. . . .

Cody shut down his feelings. He turned off his logical mind and did something ridiculous. He opened his throat and roared up at the tiger.

Brutus roared down at Cody, the sound seizing the boy's body like an electric shock.

Yell. Wave your arms. Bang against the sides of the pen. Tigers are cowards, Cody. . . . Tigers are cowards. . . .

Cody raised his rake high over his head with both hands.

Brutus loomed hugely above him, all mouth, all tongue, all dripping fangs.

Stamping his feet loudly on the ground, still roaring at the top of his lungs, Cody charged the giant carnivore.

Whatever behavior Brutus might have expected from Cody, it was clearly not this.

Brutus teetered uncertainly on his hind legs. Then he dropped to all fours.

Sensing Brutus's uncertainty on an ancient, animal level, Cody kept on coming, kept on roaring.

Brutus lowered himself to a defensive posture, belly low to the ground. Then he tensed, coiled, and prepared to spring.

Yell. Wave your arms. Bang against the sides of the pen. Tigers are cowards, Cody. . . . Tigers are cowards. . . .

Cody shrieked and shouted and banged his rake against the chain-link fence and kept walking toward the beast, stamping his feet as he got closer and closer.

Brutus roared again, baring his fangs into a contorted grimace of pure hatred. He swiped at Cody with an enormous, prong-tipped paw.

Now Cody was six feet away from the tiger.

Now five feet away.

Now four.

The animal took one tentative step backward. Then another.

Cody shouted and roared and stamped and banged his rake against the fence.

Brutus turned and trotted back through the open gate into the lockdown area.

Seeing Brutus retreat flooded Cody's body with power.

Cody sprang forward, hurling himself against the lockdown gate and clanging it shut. Then, breathing hard, he slid the locks into place.

Flushed with pure primal energy, Cody roared in victory at his defeated foe.

Brutus stood his ground on the other side of the gate and glared at Cody.

Cody stopped roaring and glared back at Brutus.

And then something strange happened.

Brutus stared at Cody in silence, and a slight shimmer surrounded the tiger, like a mini-mirage over a hot highway.

What was this shimmer? Cody had heard the word *aura* before but had never known what it meant. Now he thought it might be this shimmering he saw.

He felt that some sort of wordless understanding had passed between him and the cat. He felt a kind of mystical bond with the giant white tiger.

Eighteen

"*What in* hell was all that roaring I just heard?" Sunny demanded. She was standing, hands on hips, in an aisle between the pens.

Still flushed with victory, Cody grinned.

"Brutus somehow got out of the lockdown area while I was cleaning his pen," he said. "I know I locked him down safely. We had a little confrontation. I won." Cody's throat was raw from roaring and his voice was hoarse.

"You want to run that past me again?"

"Brutus got his shorts in a knot," said Cody. "I had to show him who was boss."

"How in hell did he get out of the lockdown area?"

she demanded. "Did I or didn't I drill you on the rules of lockdown safety?"

"Sunny, *I locked him down safely.* I did it by the book, just the way you taught me. He got out anyway."

"How?" said Sunny.

Cody lowered his voice. "Somebody must have unlocked the gate."

"What are you sayin'?"

"I think somebody unlocked the gate after I locked it," said Cody. "I think they *wanted* Brutus to attack me."

"Why?"

"I don't know," said Cody. "Maybe because they don't like me snooping around, trying to find out about Wayland."

She looked at him for a moment without speaking. Did she believe him? Did she feel guilty that his trying to help her had nearly cost him his life?

"Well," she said finally, "the important thing is you stood up to Brutus and he didn't tear you to pieces."

"Right. That's the important thing."

"I *told* you tigers were cowards, didn't I?" she said.

"Yep. That's what gave me the idea of standing up to him."

She sighed.

"You were pretty darn brave to stand up to a cat that big."

"Thanks," he said. "It's not tigers that frighten me," he added.

"Is that so?" she said. "What frightens you, Cody?"

He looked at her a moment, trying to decide how much to reveal.

"Mothers," he answered finally.

She raised her eyebrows.

"My mother is . . . a pretty scary person," he said.

"You say 'is.' Didn't you tell me she was dead?"

"It would be a lot easier if she was dead," he said.

"In what way is she scary?"

"Just living with her," he said. "Trying to read her moods. You never knew when her mood would shift and she'd suddenly become insanely angry for no reason at all. When she'd punish you for breaking some stupid little rule of hers. She had about a million stupid little rules. If you broke one of them one day, she might not even care. If you broke the same rule another day, she'd go absolutely ape."

Cody wiped perspiration from his neck and forehead.

"You know what a Ginsu kitchen knife is?" he asked. "The kind you can only buy on TV? It cuts through tin cans. It slices tomatoes so thin you can see through them. One night last February, my mother came at me with a Ginsu knife. I barricaded myself in my room. I packed all the things I really care about in my backpack. When she went to sleep, I snuck out of the apartment and hitched a ride out of the city. I've been traveling across the country ever since, working my way west. She keeps trying to bring me back."

"Is your father really dead?"

"My parents were divorced when I was five," said Cody. "My mother has always told me Dad was dead. Now I wonder. Maybe that's not true."

Sunny took off her straw cowboy hat. She wiped perspiration from her face with her arm and ran her fingers through her damp blond hair. Her T-shirt had wet spots under the arms and neck. Her tan had gotten even darker over the past few days. Cody thought she looked beautiful, scar and everything.

"You want to come inside and have a Coke or somethin'?" she asked.

Cody nodded and followed her to the house.

"So that's *my* story," said Cody. "Were your parents any better?"

She smiled sadly. She got two cans of Coke out of the fridge. She popped the top on one and handed it to him, then rolled the second one across her forehead.

"Well, I grew up on a ranch in West Texas, near a little town called Deadman. My daddy raised cattle and horses, and he talked just like Deke. He liked to compete in rodeos. He was pretty good. I wasn't too awful at it myself."

"You ever win any prizes?" Cody asked.

"Yup, when I was a teenager," she said. "Then the circus come to town. Wayland and I joined up. The trapeze was what drew me, so I trained hard and became a trapeze artist. A flier. Wayland became a tiger tamer. That's where we met Deke. One of the tigers in Wayland's act gave birth. It was the mama's first litter, so she wasn't hardly interested in nursin' 'em. Baby tigers need to be fed every four hours, and nobody at all wanted *that* job. I took those babies home to my trailer and got real good at bein' a tiger mom. Next thing I know, I've fallen in love with 'em. When the cubs got too big to keep in my trailer, the circus took 'em back, but I was hooked on the big cats."

"And you've been ranching big cats since then?"

She shook her head.

"I earned enough, workin' circuses and rodeos, to go to college," she said. "Went to the University of Texas at Austin. Majored in English and Psych. Learned how to talk proper. Then I gave that up. *Then* I started ranchin' big cats."

"Where'd you get that scar on your face?"

She touched the scar lovingly with a fingertip.

"Oh, I got gored by a bull I was ridin'," she said. "The rodeo doctor said, 'Honey, if you live to be a hundred and ten, this is the luckiest day of your natural-born life.' Cody, that horn missed my eye by an *inch*."

Nineteen

It had been hot and heavily humid all day. On the radio that morning at breakfast, there'd been talk of tornadoes in Oklahoma, of Doppler radar trackings, of a tornado watch for Texas.

Cody and Randy had spent most of the afternoon dumping dirty water out of the animals' wading pools and refilling them with fresh water. In the late afternoon the sky clouded up and it looked like a storm might be on the way.

Shortly after seven-thirty the cats became unusually restless. They paced back and forth in their pens, ill-tempered and snapping at each other. Cody and Randy were coiling up the hoses they'd used to refill the wad-

ing pools. The thickening thunderclouds in the south-
west looked strange. For one thing, they seemed to be
moving extremely fast. For another, they were greenish.
Cody couldn't ever remember seeing greenish clouds.

Warm gusts of humid air blew about the ranch. There
was a grumble of thunder in the distance. The wind
picked up and a few drops of rain splattered in the dust.

"Looks like we're going to get us a little rain," said
Randy. "We sure could use it."

A powerful gust of wind suddenly slammed Cody
against a chain-link fence.

"What the hell!" said Cody, picking up the hose he'd
dropped. "Randy, did you see that?"

"Either you weigh less than I thought, or that was
one mother of a gust," said Randy.

The tigers began to growl. The lions in Caesar's pen
began to grunt and roar, but it had a different sound
than their nightly territory-marking noises.

Thunder went ripping and tearing about the heav-
ens. Randy and Cody studied the sky.

There were flashes of lightning in the dark clouds.
Streaks of lightning shaped like delicate plant-root ten-
drils crackled across the charcoal sky.

Then the bottom of the clouds bulged like the belly
of a pregnant animal.

"Oh Lord," said Randy softly, watching the clouds.
"Please don't be what I think you are."

A sudden burst of cold rain hit them, as if someone had thrown a bucketful in their direction, then a shower of icy hailstones the size of olives. The hail hit hard enough to hurt.

The pregnant bulge in the gray thundercloud grew larger, then gave birth: what looked like an elephant's trunk slid out of the cloud and touched the ground.

"Twister!" shouted Randy. "Head for the house!"

Now they heard it: a continuous rumble, growing louder and louder, like a runaway train of boxcars hurtling toward them.

Cody dropped his hose and ran in the direction of the house. He looked back at the gray, funnel-shaped cloud. Lightning snapped to the ground around the funnel.

"C'mon, man," yelled Randy, "you do *not* want to be outside for this!"

Dust and dirt began whirling about with terrific force.

Horizontal sheets of rain hit Cody as he ran. He was completely drenched in twenty steps.

Way in the distance, Sunny appeared at the door of the ranch house.

"Twister!" she shouted. "Get in the house! Hurry!"

Another shower of hailstones hit them, these the size of golf balls. They struck Cody and Randy painfully on the head and shoulders, producing instant bruises.

Cody and Randy kept on running. The wind slammed them into the chain-link fences, then tried to drive them into the ground. They scrambled to their feet, spitting sand, and ran again.

Debris flew through the air—plastic water bowls, a rake, a shovel, sheets of plywood. Toys from Spanky's pen—a beach ball, a purple plastic hula hoop, a battered white wooden bowling pin.

A black garden hose sailed through the air, coiling and uncoiling like a sea snake.

From the left came Harlan, from the right came Deke, everybody running toward the house as fast as his legs could carry him. Cartoon characters with comically pumping arms and legs.

It was suddenly hard for Cody to breathe, hard to fill his lungs with air. A giant vacuum cleaner was sucking up all the oxygen.

The funnel cloud was tearing through the fields now, coming in their direction, churning up a swirling cloud of debris as it came.

Just fifty yards more to the house.

Now forty.

Now thirty.

"Hurry!" yelled Sunny. "Run faster!"

Something smacked Cody hard on the back of his head and wrapped itself around his neck. Another hose. He tore it off his neck and flung it into the air. It sailed upward and disappeared.

More freezing rain, more icy hail. Just twenty more yards to the house.

Now fifteen.

Now ten.

Now five.

Randy, followed by Cody, dove for the door, followed by Harlan and Deke.

They tumbled breathlessly into the house, piling on top of each other like clowns in a circus. The door slammed shut.

"We made it!" shouted Randy.

"I can't believe we made it!" Cody gasped.

They picked themselves up and dusted themselves off, combing sand and ice balls out of their hair. Cody was relieved to be able to fill his lungs with air again after the vacuum he'd left behind.

Outside, the wind tore and tugged at the house, trying to tease it apart.

"What about the animals?" Cody asked.

"Whyn't you go back out there and bring 'em in the house, boy?" said Deke. "I bet we got room for at least a dozen tigers in here."

The tiger babies, Mary Jane and Sniffles, woke from

all the noise and waddled into the living room to be fed. Sunny went to get baby bottles and formula.

The wind outside had increased in force. Hammers, screwdrivers, buckets, and tenpenny nails shot through the air like guided missiles and slammed into the house.

Cody looked out a window in time to see something huge, striped, and four-legged fly through the air. He could have sworn it was a tiger.

Somewhere, another window shattered in a shower of glass.

Something heavy landed on the roof.

"Please don't let that be an animal," said Sunny softly, returning with formula and baby bottles.

It grew dark as night. Sunny started turning on lights.

The freight-train noise grew louder. Nobody spoke. Nobody would have heard them if they had.

There was a painfully bright flash of lightning and a shattering crack of thunder. An instant later all the lights winked out.

"Great," said Sunny.

"Where's the storm cellar?" Cody asked.

Everybody laughed.

"We don't *got* no steenking storm cellar," said Deke in a Mexican accent. "You theenk there ees time to *deeg* one, senor?"

"So what do we do if the tornado hits the house?" Cody asked.

"Fly away," said Deke. "Spread our wings and fly away to Heaven."

Deke flapped his arms. Everybody laughed again.

"Seriously, y'all," said Sunny. "Stay away from the windows and move toward the center of the house."

Nobody moved. *Too macho to do anything like that,* Cody thought. *Although not too macho to have dived into the house like frightened schoolgirls.*

Deke took out his cigarette lighter and flicked it on. Sunny went into the kitchen and came back with flashlights and a tray of votive candles. Deke lit the candles with his lighter.

Something heavy slammed into a wall outside.

"Isn't there anything we can do for the animals?" Cody asked.

"No," said Sunny. "My poor babies. They must be so scared."

While the wind shrieked and wailed, Sunny and Cody nursed Mary Jane and Sniffles from the baby bottles, then burped them. The cubs waddled back to the closet to sleep, unaware of the tornado and too young to be afraid.

Within fifteen minutes, it all stopped.

Things no longer flew through the air. The wind died down. Even the rain stopped. There was no sound outside. It was eerily quiet.

Cautiously, Sunny opened the door and looked outside.

"Oh my God," she said.

"What is it?" Cody asked.

He stepped through the doorway and looked. Trees had fallen, giant roots ripped right out of the earth. Power lines lay broken on the ground, showers of sparks pouring out of them. The field just beyond the pens was lined with flames.

"Fire!" said Sunny.

Deke and Harlan ran into the kitchen. They returned with two large fire extinguishers and raced out to the field.

Sunny punched out a number on the speakerphone.

"Saddler's Creek Fire Department," said a voice.

"This is Sunny Carter up at the Sam Houston Tiger Ranch. We got a field on fire behind us and the flames are headin' our way. How soon can y'all get out here?"

"It's gonna be at least an hour, ma'am."

"An *hour*!" said Sunny. "You don't understand. This fire is threatening the lives of sixty-six of my big cats."

"I'm sorry, ma'am," said the voice. "We got a limited number of firefighters. We got our hands full with fires right here in Saddler's Creek."

"Okay," said Sunny, "unless y'all come out here immediately, the only way I can save my lions and tigers is to set 'em free. That's sixty-six lions and tigers loose in the fields."

There was no immediate response from the other end of the line. Then:

"We're on our way, ma'am."

Sunny, Randy, and Cody grabbed flashlights and ran outside.

In the dark it was hard to see exactly what had happened. There was debris everywhere. The Mule was upside down on the garage roof. The screen door on the front of the house had been torn off. So had most of the shingles, the satellite dish on the roof, and part of the roof itself. The windows on the front of the house were smashed. The back of the house had been ripped away and had simply disappeared.

Two large sheds were gone. The silver Airstream trailer that Deke lived in was still there, but the trailer that used to stand next to it had disappeared. Cody didn't see how a tornado could send one trailer hurtling into the air till it vanished and leave the one right beside it completely untouched.

The animals were in a frenzy, flinging themselves against the chain-link fences, growling, roaring, hysterical with fear.

Cody counted three downed power lines, sparking like Fourth of July firecrackers.

Judging by the damage, a small, intense tornado

had come in at an angle and hit the corner pens before veering off sharply in another direction.

The pens of Siegfried and Roy, of Horace and Boris and Chewy and Chomper, of the leopards Kiko and Kamara, and of Spanky the lion were nothing but twisted metal. The front wall of Brutus's pen was flattened. All of these animals were now gone.

Deke and Harlan ran back with the fire extinguishers.

"These things are useless against a brush fire," said Deke. "Are the hose jockeys comin' out?"

"They'll be here in about twenty minutes," said Sunny. "Gentlemen, we've got us a problem. We've got a lion, two leopards, and seven tigers missin'. They're either dead or they're loose and completely freaked out. We're each goin' to arm ourselves with a rake, a torch, and a leash, and we're goin' to find 'em. If they're dead, we need to know that. If they're alive, we need to round 'em up and lock 'em down before they kill somebody. This is extremely dangerous work. If you'd prefer not to do it, tell me now and it's fine, but I do need to know right now. Anybody not want to do this?"

Cody, Randy, Harlan, and Deke exchanged wary glances and remained silent.

"Good," she said. "Thank you. Okay, gentlemen, let's get started."

Twenty

Working together, torches held high, Cody and Randy searched the area in back of the house and around the sheds and the swimming pool. They were looking for any animals that might be hiding there. They knew that at any moment, a frightened tiger or leopard could leap out at them and kill them.

"Watch my back, man," said Randy, poking his torch behind sheds and into corners.

"I got yours," said Cody. "Just don't take your eyes off *mine.*"

They made their way cautiously across the grounds, aware that they were probably being watched, alert for the slightest movement, flinching at shadows thrown by the flickering torches.

"I hate this," said Randy. "The suspense, I mean."

"I know," said Cody.

"I hate not knowin' when somethin's gonna drop down on top of me and tear my face off. I'd much rather a cat jumped on me right now and got it over with."

"I know what you mean," said Cody.

They crept forward, swiveling their heads from side to side like radar antennas, trying to pick up the faintest sound of a cat about to spring.

Up ahead were yards of torn and crunched-up corrugated tin that had been ripped off a shed. Three or four tigers or leopards could be crouching beneath it now, waiting to attack.

"This must be what it's like to be on night patrol in a war," said Cody.

"I'd rather be shot than have my face tore off by a leopard," said Randy.

They circled the pile of corrugated tin, holding their torches in one hand, their rakes in the other.

"You see anything?" Cody whispered.

"No," whispered Randy.

Just then they heard something. A slight creaking from somewhere above.

"Shhhhhh," said Randy.

They looked upward and saw nothing but branches of trees, silhouetted against the night sky.

Then something came crashing down behind them, and both boys jumped three feet into the air.

It was a giant tree limb, weakened by the tornado, nothing more. It missed them by about a foot.

"Close one," said Cody.

In the distance they heard the gradual approach of sirens. Cody hoped it was the fire engines from Saddler's Creek.

"Those firemen sure ain't gonna come on the property if they think we got loose tigers," said Randy.

"We'd better go see if we can help," said Cody.

By the time Randy and Cody got out to County Road 2433 by the main gate, Sunny, Deke, and Harlan were already there. The fire vehicles were just pulling up.

"The fire is in the field behind the pens!" Sunny shouted.

"We see it," said the captain. "How close can we get to the field?"

"Hang a left onto the property and then a right," said Deke. "When you can't go no further, it's another twenty yards past the pens."

"Your tigers are all locked up, though, right?" asked the captain.

Sunny looked at Deke.

"Pretty much," said Sunny.

"Pretty much?" said the captain. "Meaning not all the tigers are locked up?"

"One or two might have got out durin' the tornado," said Sunny. "My men will run interference for you."

The captain looked at Deke, Harlan, Randy, and Cody.

"Those rakes are going to protect us from tigers?"

"Rakes and torches," said Sunny. "Can't get any better'n that. C'mon."

The fire vehicles drove as far as the pens, the tiger wranglers trotting behind them with rakes and torches. The fire had spread to the edge of the field. Clouds of smoke and cinders blew into the nearest pens.

The firemen hopped off their engines. They unfolded yards of flat white canvas hose from the engines and pulled it down the aisles, stretching it between the pens.

The tigers in the pens roared at them as they passed, some leaping to a standing position on their hind legs, hanging on to the tops of the fences with their claws.

"Holy Mo!" said one fireman. "Will you look at that?"

"It's not the ones *inside* the pens you need to worry about," said Deke with a wicked smile.

"Thanks a lot, Pops," said the fireman.

The men who'd remained on the engines started pumping water into the flat hoses from the holding tanks. The hoses filled and fattened. The firemen adjusted the brass nozzles and began shooting water at the flames.

The fire that threatened the pens was soon knocked down to a smoking sizzle. The firemen went to work next on the downed power lines, disconnecting them and quenching the showers of sparks.

"How soon do y'all think we can get our power back on?" Sunny asked the captain.

"You'll have to check with your local power company on that one, ma'am," said the fire captain. "We're fire-fighters. All we do is knock 'em down and put 'em out."

The firemen drained their hoses flat, folded them up, put them back onto the trucks, and began backing and turning their vehicles out of the tiger ranch.

"Thanks, guys!" Sunny shouted as the trucks pulled out.

The captain leaned out of the cab of his truck.

"Now that it don't matter," he said, "was there any more than two tigers on the loose?"

"Oh, *lots* more than two," said Sunny cheerily. "Thanks again!"

The moment the fire engines pulled out, everyone resumed searching for escaped animals. Cody and Randy continued their hunt behind the house and around the sheds.

The clouds were melting away, and the moon was brightening the night and illuminating their search.

Cody glanced up at the roof of the house, which was piled with debris. He could make out the shapes of objects: a lawn chair, a bucket, a shovel, a wheelbarrow . . .

The clouds soon disappeared altogether. The moon, nearly full, bathed the ranch in bluish white light.

"Oh no," said Cody.

"What is it?" Randy asked.

"Up there. On the roof."

Randy looked.

"A tiger," said Randy. "A dead one."

"You sure it's dead?"

"It sure *looks* dead," said Randy. "From the way it's lyin'."

"During the tornado, I looked out the window," said Cody. "I thought I saw a tiger flying through the air. I couldn't believe it."

Randy put down his rake and handed Cody his torch. Then he walked up to the house, found a foothold on a sill, and climbed up onto the roof. He stood looking down at the tiger.

"He's dead all right," said Randy sadly.

"Who is it, can you tell?" Cody asked.

"Siegfried, I think."

"Poor Siegfried," said Cody.

"We'll have to tell Sunny," said Randy. He climbed down from the roof.

Cody handed the torch back to Randy and then something caught his eye. Two glowing eyes were watching them from a bush. Cody gripped his rake tightly.

"Look over there," Cody whispered. "Between the shed and the garage."

Randy looked.

"You see two glowing eyes?" Cody whispered.

"Yeah."

"What do we do now?" Cody whispered.

"I don't know."

"You don't know?"

"To be honest with you, I never actually had to deal with an escaped cat before," Randy whispered.

"Great."

Cody dropped his torch on the ground, stamped out the flames, and began moving slowly toward the glowing eyes.

"What're you doin'?" Randy whispered.

"Shhhhh," said Cody.

Knowing animals' fear of fire, Cody figured he had a better chance of approaching this cat—whoever it was—without a torch. Slowly, slowly, Cody made his way closer to the glowing eyes.

"Fff-fff-fff-fff-fff," Cody chuffed softly. "Fff-fff-fff-fff-fff."

He was almost up to the bush. The glowing eyes

never moved. Maybe the animal didn't realize Cody saw him. Cody wondered who it was—Roy? Chomper? Chewy? He hoped it wasn't Brutus. He didn't feel up to another roaring contest with Brutus.

He could now make out the form of the animal that crouched behind the bush. It wasn't large. There were no stripes. Cody put down his rake.

"Spanky," said Cody. "How ya doing, buddy?"

The young lion let himself be petted, let his face be roughly scrubbed with Cody's fingernails. Then he came out from behind the bush and fell against Cody's legs before climbing on his lap and licking his face with a rough tongue.

"Good *boy*, Spanky," said Cody. "Good *boy!*"

Randy came forward with a leash and snapped it on to Spanky's collar.

"Okay, buddy," said Randy, "we're goin' back to the pens now. We're goin' to find you a nice, safe place to spend the night."

Cody pushed Spanky off his lap and got to his feet, but when Randy tugged on the leash, Spanky wouldn't move.

"C'mon, Spanky," said Randy. "Let's go, good buddy."

"Let me try it," said Cody.

He took the leash and gave it a gentle tug. Spanky lay down on the ground and rolled over on his back.

Cody remembered Deke saying lions were stubborn and didn't see why they had to walk on a leash.

"Maybe if we both pulled him," Cody suggested.

They began to pull on the leash, dragging Spanky along the ground.

"This isn't good," said Randy.

"You're right."

Together they grabbed Spanky and carried him toward the pens. Despite the weight he'd lost from not eating, Spanky still weighed 150 pounds. They couldn't carry him for long, so they put him back down on the ground. He just let himself be dragged, like a dead animal. It took them a while to get him to the pens. Working carefully, they put him into the lockdown area of another cat's pen.

As they were locking Spanky down, Deke jogged past them. He was carrying a gun—his heavy .45-caliber automatic pistol.

"Where are you going?" Cody called.

"A neighbor just phoned!" Deke yelled. "He seen Brutus over by the ranch next door! He's got him a eight-year-old boy cornered there!"

"You mean Arthur?"

"He didn't give me no names. That tiger shouldn't even be alive. I'm gonna blow a hole in him you can drive a truck through!"

Twenty-one

"Wait!" Cody shouted. "I'm coming with you!"

"Stay *out* of this, son. This is between me and Brutus."

Deke took off across the field in the direction of the neighbor's ranch. Cody ran and caught up with him.

"I said stay *out* of this," said Deke.

"But I want to help."

"If you really wanna help," said Deke, "get lost!"

Cody felt suddenly protective of the beast he'd stood up to.

"Don't shoot him, Deke," Cody pleaded. "Please. I know how to handle him."

"So do I. Now get the hell outta my way!"

"I'm coming with you," said Cody.

"It's a free country," said Deke.

Deke and Cody ran through the field, matching strides. The tall field grass whipped their faces as they ran. Cody was in good shape and could run for miles. What shape could Deke be in at age seventy, especially with all that smoking?

Three-quarters of the way across the field, Deke began coughing, which slowed him down.

Cody kept going. He felt a bond with the big tiger since their face-off in the pen. He had no idea what he'd do when he saw the tiger; he just knew he had to stop Deke from shooting him. If Brutus had already attacked Arthur, it would be hard to do that, and he might not even try. But if, by some miracle, the boy was still alive, then maybe Cody would have a chance.

Cody slowed down, not because he was winded but because he figured he had to be close to where Brutus had the boy cornered. It wouldn't be good to startle them.

He moved through the tall grass as quietly as he could, stopping every few steps to listen. He heard nothing except normal night sounds—crickets, cicadas, katydids, bugs that sounded like a ratchet tool being twisted back and forth.

He could hear Deke behind him, running through the field, breathing hard and coughing. Now Deke must have sensed that stealth was preferable, for he, too, slowed down and got quiet.

Cody could see the ranch house over the tops of the weeds. Maybe Arthur and the tiger were close to the house. Cody took a step and listened. He took another step and listened. He took another step, and suddenly, in the light of the almost-full moon, he saw them.

About ten feet ahead and to the left. The huge white tiger had his back to Cody, but he'd turned his head around to look at him. Arthur was just beyond the tiger, frozen in place.

Brutus looked more puzzled than angry. His ears weren't flattened, his teeth weren't bared, and he wasn't snarling.

"Arthur, are you coming in now or aren't you?" called a woman's voice from the house.

The tiger's ears swiveled in the direction of the voice, but the rest of him remained motionless. The eight-year-old boy was a statue.

"Answer me, Arthur, or you'll be sorry!" called the voice.

Arthur and the tiger remained absolutely still.

"If you don't get in here this minute," called the voice, "I'm gonna hafta come out there and get you!"

No one moved.

Then Cody heard a soft sound behind him and saw the tiger's ears go flat. He knew that Deke had crept up behind him. He knew that Deke now had the automatic aimed just past him at the tiger. Did the tiger know what guns were? Probably not.

Cody knew how tricky this situation was. The great white tiger had Arthur in front of him and Cody behind him. Deke was behind Cody, and Deke's pistol was pointed at the tiger. If Cody turned toward Deke, his back would be to Brutus and the tiger would leap on him.

Cody prayed that the woman who was calling Arthur wouldn't make good on her threat to come out here. One unexpected sound now, one unexpected movement, and the delicate balance would collapse.

Cody realized he'd stopped breathing and willed himself to start again.

"Slowly sink to your knees, Cody," said Deke in a quiet, steady voice. "I need me a clear shot here."

Cody didn't move.

He had already begged Deke not to shoot, and the message hadn't gotten through. He knew that any second now, a shot from Deke's automatic could tear open the back of his head.

Cody could hear a sliding screen door being pulled back. Could hear sandy steps on the flagstones of the patio. Could hear swishing strides in the tall grass, coming toward them.

Cody honestly didn't know what he was going to say or do next, but he had felt braver since confronting Brutus in his pen, and he knew that the time had come to act. He shut down his feelings.

"Arthur," said Cody in the same quiet, steady voice that Deke had used, "I am going to take the tiger home now. Do not move and do not make a sound."

Cody took a slow-motion step in the direction of the tiger.

The tiger's lips drew back from his teeth, but he made no sound.

Cody took another slow-motion step in the tiger's direction.

The growl began deep inside the tiger's chest.

Cody took another slow-motion step in the tiger's direction.

The tiger's face contorted into a nose-wrinkling snarl of rage.

Cody took another slow-motion step in the tiger's direction. He slowly held out his right hand toward Brutus's nose so the tiger could sniff it, inspect it, or bite it off if he chose.

Snarling, Brutus sniffed the hand. Cody could feel the tiger's hot breath burning his wrist.

Slowly, slowly, slowly, Cody's hand went toward the tiger's throat.

His fingertips touched the tiger's collar.

Slowly, slowly, slowly, a millimeter at a time, Cody's fingers closed around the tiger's heavy leather collar.

"Good boy, Brutus," Cody whispered. "Good boy. Please, Deke, Arthur. Nobody move. Please."

Cody tugged gently at the tiger's collar. It was like tugging at a post.

"Good boy, Brutus," Cody whispered again. "We're going home now, boy."

Cody tugged harder, expecting that at any moment the massive jaws would clamp together on his wrist and separate it from his arm.

Amazingly, he felt the tiger's resistance slacken.

"Good boy, Brutus," Cody whispered again, and pulled a little harder.

The tiger's resistance slackened more. And even more. Amazingly, the giant beast seemed to be allowing Cody to lead him.

Slowly, slowly, Cody turned around.

Deke was five feet away, his heavy, flat steel automatic pistol pointed at them, extended in a two-handed shooter's grip. Deke's right hand was closed around the handle of the gun, resting it on his left palm.

Slowly, slowly, slowly, Cody pulled the tiger toward Deke, and toward Deke, and toward Deke, and then *past* Deke.

Cody prayed that the angry ex-Marine would hold

his fire. He prayed that Deke wouldn't make any sudden sounds or movements. He thought he heard Deke start to follow them.

Slowly, slowly, slowly, Cody advanced across the field, leading the eight-hundred-pound Siberian tiger by the collar, speaking quietly and reassuringly to him, chuffing to him, talking to him in his native tongue.

It was a little like his daytime walks with Chomper. *Very* little like his daytime walks with Chomper. Brutus was four times as big and eight times as dangerous.

They kept walking across the field. Cody must have been breathing, must have had a heartbeat, but he wasn't aware of either. The swish of their movement through the tall grass was the only sound. Even the bugs seemed to have stopped their chirping and ratcheting.

When Cody and Brutus, followed by Deke, came out of the field and into the Sam Houston Tiger Ranch, Sunny saw them walking toward her and she froze. When they passed her, she got in line behind Deke. It was a strange procession.

They passed Randy and they passed Harlan, and each of them froze as well.

Cody had absolutely no idea what he was going to do with Brutus next.

"Hold him there a moment if you can," called Sunny softly. "We're goin' to find you a pen to put him in."

Cody stopped Brutus. Out of the corner of his eye, Cody saw Sunny, Harlan, Randy, and Deke creep quietly around the far side of the pens.

Sensing Brutus, the tigers in the nearest pens began to growl. Brutus growled in response. His ears went flat and his lips drew back.

"It's okay, Brutus, they can't hurt you," Cody whispered. He scratched the tiger's enormous face with his free hand, as he had done with Chomper many times before.

Working quickly, Sunny and the others shuttled animals to different pens—doubling up tigers who knew each other in the same pens, clearing out one pen big enough for Brutus by himself.

Within minutes, Cody was able to lead Brutus in his new pen. Nobody else dared to come close to the giant tiger, so Cody did the entire lockdown procedure by himself.

When he finished, Sunny, Harlan, Deke, and Randy gave him a round of applause.

Cody blushed and felt his body begin to let go of all its stored-up tension.

"I bet you think you're hot stuff now," said Deke. "A real cowboy."

"Where in the name of all that's holy did you ever get the guts to do that?" Randy demanded.

"I don't know," said Cody.

"What were you thinkin' the whole time?" Sunny asked.

"That I didn't want to die," said Cody. "That I didn't want Brutus to die."

"Nice work, kid," said Harlan.

"Thanks," said Cody.

Twenty-two

The animals didn't understand what had happened, but it made them angry. They snapped and snarled at everybody and were in an ugly mood.

Sunny spent time with each cat, calming, chuffing, soothing grouchy tempers, trying to push down her own suffocating sadness over the deaths of her animals.

Victims of the tornado were the two white tigers Siegfried and Roy, and both leopards, Kiko and Kamara. Once Sunny identified the bodies, the wranglers spared her further contact with them. She quickly removed all their baby pictures from the sides of the refrigerator—two-week-old Siegfried and Roy nursing from baby bottles, three-week-old Kiko and Kamara sleeping in her slippers—and threw them into the trash.

Miraculously, the gang had found the young tigers—Chomper, Chewy, Horace, and Boris—hanging out together near the swimming pool. The wranglers had returned them to the pens while Cody was busy with Brutus.

Cleanup began at dawn. Severely damaged structures and fallen trees were dismantled with gas-powered chain saws and hauled away. All debris from the tornado was collected at the carrion pits and then burned or buried, or both. The magnified whine of chain saws and the stench of burning rubble filled the day. The Mule, once it was lifted down from the garage roof and placed firmly on the ground, started chugging immediately.

Repairing the pens took precedence over all other activities, and every member of the staff took an active role in rebuilding them. At Sunny's request, the loss of the four animals wasn't discussed further.

At noon Arthur and his mother came over with gifts of beef and beer. Arthur gave Cody his baseball glove, personally autographed by Alex Rodriguez when he was a shortstop for the Texas Rangers.

"Hey, buddy, what's *this* for?" Cody asked.

"S-s-s-saving my l-l-l-life," said Arthur, suddenly bashful and unable to look at the older boy.

"Well, thanks, Arthur, but I think you should keep this."

Arthur shook his head violently from side to side. "N-n-n-no, it's f-f-f-for *you*! If you don't w-w-w-want it, I'll th-th-th-throw it away!"

Surprised by the kid's passion and anxious not to insult him, Cody took the glove.

By five p.m. the power company truck drove up, and by eight p.m. their electricity was on again.

The next week, after his rebuilding activities, Cody worked with Mary Jane and Sniffles, feeding them, burping them, and teaching them not to bite or scratch.

Cody was shoveling poop in Spanky's pen when Arthur showed up, carrying a white plastic bag from the supermarket.

"Hey, Arthur," said Cody, "what've you got there?"

"T-t-treats for S-S-Spanky," said Arthur. "L-l-look how s-s-scrawny he's g-g-gettin'. Y-y-you c-c-can s-s-see his ribs. He's 'bout as th-th-thin as a b-b-bat's ear."

"He's lost way too much weight," said Cody, frowning. "We've got to get him to eat some solid food."

Arthur opened his bag and took out a spoon and a dozen small jars of baby food.

"Hey, S-S-Spanky, see what I b-b-brung you?" said Arthur. "A whole l-l-lot of different f-f-flavors. M-m-maybe one of th-th-these is s-s-somethin' you l-l-like."

Arthur twisted the lid off a tiny glass jar of baby

food—broccoli, chicken, and wild rice. He dipped the spoon into it and lifted the spoon to Spanky's mouth.

"F-f-f-first, w-w-what do you th-th-think of th-th-*this*?"

Spanky sniffed at the broccoli, chicken, and wild rice, then pushed it away with his nose. Arthur wiped off the spoon and dipped it into another jar.

"N-n-next we have th-th-*this*," he said.

Arthur dipped the spoon into the jar of carrots, beef, and barley, and lifted it to Spanky's nose.

Spanky sniffed at the carrots, beef, and barley. Then he pushed it away with his nose.

Arthur wiped off the spoon and dipped it into a jar of lasagna with meat sauce.

Spanky sniffed at the lasagna with meat sauce and pushed it away with his nose.

Arthur wiped off the spoon and dipped it into sweet potatoes and turkey, turkey and rice, chicken and rice, chicken and noodles, chicken and pears, chicken and apples, apples and ham, and carrots and beef, and Spanky pushed them all away with his nose. But when Arthur dipped his spoon into spaghetti with mini meatballs, Spanky sniffed it, licked it, and gobbled it up.

"He l-l-l-*likes* it!" Arthur shouted. "He l-l-l-*likes* it!"

So Spanky began eating solid food again. But for a long time, he would only eat Gerber-brand spaghetti with mini meatballs.

Twenty-three

With all the work created by the tornado, Cody didn't get a chance to follow up at the Heartbreak Motel until a few nights later. He drove Sunny's pickup truck back to Saddler's Creek and parked outside the motel's office.

The Heartbreak Motel was a cheesy little place built in the 1950s and later renamed and redecorated to give it a new look. There were several signed and framed pictures of Elvis. There was an electric guitar and a sequined jumpsuit on display, but it was doubtful that the King had ever touched either of these.

The regular night clerk, a man named Clint, had a shaved head and a heavy black mustache. "Help you?" asked Clint.

"Yes, sir," said Cody. "I'm looking for a friend of mine, Wayland Carter? I was told he might be staying here."

Cody handed him Wayland's picture. Clint took out a pair of gold-rimmed reading glasses and examined the photo. Then he gave it back without comment.

"So how'd you make out in the twister?" Clint asked.

"It could've been worse," said Cody.

"With a twister it could *always* be worse," said Clint, sipping coffee from a plastic mug with his name on it.

"Right," said Cody. "So tell me. Does the guy in the photo look at all familiar to you?"

"Can't say for sure," said Clint.

"If you can't say for sure, can you at least say it's possible?"

"Maybe," said Clint.

"Maybe?"

"And then again, maybe not," said Clint. "My memory's a little foggy."

"I see."

"Do you?" said Clint.

"Do I what?"

"See?"

"Yes," said Cody. "I mean no. I mean . . . *what*?"

"Do you see that my memory's a little foggy?"

"Oh, uh, yeah," said Cody.

There was something fishy going on here. Clint

seemed to be saying something without saying it. And then Cody got it: Of course. The desk clerk was asking for a bribe!

Cody didn't know much about bribes. The only time he'd ever seen a bribe offered to anybody was when he once watched an old British movie on TV. A man in a tuxedo pulled a bill out of his pocket and thrust it at a sleazy-looking guy in a bar, exclaiming, "Well then, perhaps *this* will refresh your memory!"

Cody kept a five-dollar bill in his right front pocket. He yanked it out and thrust it awkwardly at the night clerk.

"Well then, perhaps *this* will refresh your memory!" said Cody. He hadn't noticed that the five-dollar bill was old and as fragile as Kleenex and that when he yanked it out of his jeans, it tore and the other half remained in his pocket.

Clint took one look at the torn bill and erupted in laughter, spitting coffee.

"For half a five, kid," he said, "I couldn't remember my *mama's* name."

"How much would it take to bring back your memory?" Cody asked.

"A Benjamin might bring it all back to me."

"A what?" said Cody.

"A Benjamin Franklin. A hundred-dollar bill."

"A hundred dollars?" said Cody. "I don't have any-where *near* a hundred dollars."

"How much *do* you have?"

Cody emptied his pockets on the checkout desk and counted out what he had. There were folded bills and crumpled ones. There was quite a lot of small change.

"Sixty-seven dollars and forty-two cents," said Cody finally.

"Okay, son," said Clint, "we're having a post-tornado sale tonight. A Benjamin's worth of memory for just sixty-seven forty-two." The desk clerk scooped up all of Cody's money. "The fella in your photo there did stay here a couple nights two weeks ago," he said, "but he ain't here no more. And he didn't leave no forwarding address."

"Can I see how he signed the register?"

"Why not?" said Clint.

The desk clerk opened the register and went a few pages back. He pointed.

"Here it is. See? He signed it 'Wayne Cash.'"

"Wayne Cash" for "Wayland Carter." The hand-writing will prove it's the same person.

Cody got back to the ranch and told Sunny what he had found. She gave him a huge hug.

"Oh, by the way," said Sunny, "while you were gone, you got a call."

"I did?" said Cody. "Who was it?"

"I dunno, hon," said Sunny. "Some woman, didn't leave her name. She sounded real nice, though."

Who could have called him? Nobody knew he was here. Well, there was Mitch, of course, back at Dusty's Tex-Mex, but Mitch sure wasn't a woman. And then it hit him: *His mother had tracked him as far as the tiger ranch.*

Twenty-four

When Cody phoned Detective Runyon in Dallas the following morning and told him about Wayne Cash, Runyon was less impressed than Cody had hoped he'd be.

"But this is *important*," said Cody. "Wayland Carter isn't dead! He stayed at the Heartbreak Motel just two weeks ago!"

"No, son," said Runyon, "*Wayne Cash* stayed at the Heartbreak Motel two weeks ago."

"And they're the same person!" said Cody.

"That has not been determined," said Runyon. "Look, son, I'll go to this motel and check out your lead, but it won't mean spit unless that Wayne Cash signature is analyzed by a graphologist and found to be the same handwriting as Wayland Carter's. And that's a mighty big *unless.*"

Cody hung up the phone.

If Wayland was alive, then whoever planted his bloody shirt in the carrion pits did it to frame Sunny for murder. With Sunny in prison, Wayland would finally be free to sell the ranch. If Cody could somehow get into Deke's trailer and look around, maybe he could find something about the sale.

It would be stupid and risky to sneak into Deke's trailer to look around. Even if Deke was off somewhere working, he could come back at any moment. Cody shuddered to think how angry Deke would be to find Cody snooping through his things. It would be much too dangerous.

After breakfast the visiting vet arrived. When Deke and the vet drove off on the Mule to vaccinate the residents of the lion compound, Cody slipped into the trailer.

The metal vehicle was an oven in the hot sun. It stank of stale beer and squashed-out cigarettes. Empty bottles of Jack Daniel's Tennessee whiskey and Corona beer and articles of discarded clothing covered every horizontal surface. Cody wondered how anybody could stand living in such a sloppy, smelly place.

He began to rummage around.

Deke was a slob in most of his personal habits, although not in his business correspondence. In the bottom drawer of a white metal filing cabinet in the trailer was a neatly arranged series of papers. There were invoices from a lumberyard, from the garage that repaired the Mule, from suppliers of chain-link fencing. There were letters from neighbors who felt threatened by the presence of the big cats, and letters in response from Deke.

There were angry letters from People for the Ethical Treatment of Animals, which complained that the cats at the ranch were being treated inhumanely, although Cody doubted that anybody from PETA had ever been here.

There were letters from the United States Department of Agriculture. The USDA had received a complaint from somebody who'd posed for a photo with a baby tiger at the ranch and claimed she'd been scratched. She was threatening a major lawsuit. There was correspondence with a lawyer about this.

There seemed to be nothing suspicious. Cody was just about to give up when something caught his eye. A letter from a company called ValCom, dated a week ago. It began:

Dear Mr. Halligan:
We are delighted to learn that there is no longer any resistance from Ms. Carter and that our proposal to

purchase the Sam Houston Tiger Ranch can now proceed. . . .

How could Deke have told anyone a week ago that there'd no longer be resistance from Sunny? He couldn't have. Unless . . . unless he already knew she'd be out of the way because he'd set it up himself.

Suddenly Cody heard the sound of the Mule's engine approaching. He peeked out the window of the trailer. Deke and the vet were in the Mule, talking and laughing, headed this way!

Cody hastily stuffed all the papers back into the white metal filing cabinet, slid the drawer shut, opened the door, slipped around the far side of the trailer, and hid in the high weeds.

Had they seen him? Probably not. They were too involved in whatever they were talking about, and they were on the opposite side of the door he'd gone out of.

"I found a letter in Deke's trailer," said Cody. "I think it proves that Deke and Wayland were trying to frame Sunny for Wayland's murder."

Both Randy and Harlan groaned. It was night and his two bunkmates were watching another police reality show on the bunkhouse TV.

"You want to hear my theory?" Cody asked.

"Do we have to?" said Randy.

"Yes. Listen to this. After Sunny refused to sell the ranch, Deke and Wayland were furious at her, okay? They wanted her out of the way, where she couldn't block the sale. They didn't want to kill her, but they didn't mind sending her to prison. So they decided to try and frame her for Wayland's murder. They buried Wayland's shirt in the carrion pits, then they tipped off the Dallas police."

"How'd Wayland's shirt get all that blood on it?" asked Randy, never taking his eyes off the screen.

"He cut himself and squeezed out enough of his blood on it so the cops could test it and see it was his," said Cody.

"Cody," said Randy, "everybody knows what a huge crush you got on that woman. Why can't you just accept the fact she killed her brother to save the cats? Why can't you just accept that?"

Twenty-five

The relentlessly hot weather had returned. The rays of the sun seared Cody's skin as if focused through a magnifying glass.

Deke and Cody were cleaning Brutus's recently repaired pen. Deke had put Brutus in the lockdown area. He was now holding the shovel and Cody was raking in the crap.

"So, Cody, I hear you got a theory Sunny was framed," said Deke.

"Excuse me?"

"I hear you got a theory maybe I framed Sunny," said Deke.

"Who told you that?" Cody silently cursed Randy and Harlan.

"Is that your theory, boy?"

Why the hell had Randy and Harlan blabbed to Deke what he'd told them? Were they in on the plot to frame Sunny, too?

"I never had any idea about who framed Sunny," said Cody.

"But you're sure workin' on one *now,* ain't you?" said Deke.

"No, not really."

"No?" said Deke. "Hey, boy, I'll believe that when there's whales in West Texas. So, outside of the mess, how'd you like my old Airstream?"

"What?"

"My trailer. If you hadn't took off so fast, we coulda had us a couple beers. Kicked back, chewed the fat, maybe swapped a few theories of framin'."

Cody just stared at him, unable to think of a thing to say. Okay, so Deke knew Cody had been in his trailer. So Deke knew Cody thought he had framed Sunny. So big deal. He'd never go so far as trying to kill Cody to shut him up, would he? Only a *crazy* guy would do that. A really angry, *crazy* guy. Deke wasn't *that* crazy, was he?

"You nervous, boy? You look as jumpy as spit on a hot skillet."

With a sly smile, Deke reached into a pocket of his jeans. He took out a jackknife, fiddled with it a moment, and idly flipped out the blade. He breathed on the blade and buffed it on his shirt. He looked at his reflection in the blade and made a comical face. Then, still smiling, he waved it in the air, barely brushing Cody's hand.

A thin thread of red blood appeared on Cody's hand. The cut was so fine Cody didn't even feel it. Deke's action had seemed so casual, so empty of emotion, it took a moment to appreciate that Deke was about to kill him.

Once more, everything in Cody's universe cranked down to slow motion, the way it had when Brutus charged him on his hind legs. The image of Deke in front of him was like an overexposed photograph: The sunlit parts had grown painfully bright, the parts in shadow were utterly black. All the middle tones had bleached out and disappeared.

Cody was no match for the highly trained ex-Marine, no matter what the guy's age. This man knew martial arts. This man had been schooled in hand-to-hand combat. This man was an expert in fighting with knives. What chance did a fourteen-year-old boy have against a man like this?

Cody started to back away from Deke, then stopped.

If you didn't back away from tigers, you didn't back away from Deke. Besides, the only way out of the pen was behind Deke. If Cody backed up, he'd be trapped against the chain-link fence.

Cody's heart was hammering in his chest. It felt like his shirt was way too tight. There was no room to expand his chest, to fill his lungs with air. He could scarcely breathe. He tried to shut down his feelings. Cody grabbed his rake with both hands and held it out in front of him horizontally.

Deke chuckled at Cody's pitiful attempt at a defense. Cody felt like a fool. A fool who was about to die.

Behind Deke, something caught Cody's eye. Deke must have been careless about the lockdown door again, because Brutus had managed to nudge it open with his massive head.

The huge white tiger silently padded into the pen behind Deke.

Brutus stared at Cody, holding his gaze as if communicating something. The boy no longer felt the slightest fear of the giant white tiger. And he saw no reason to warn Deke that Brutus was standing right behind him.

Deke again swiped his blade at Cody.

Though Cody tried to block the attack with his rake, Deke was too fast for him. Cody's forearm was slashed now, blood welling up in the cut.

Frenzied emergency messages flooded his mind:

Stop the bleeding! Put pressure on the wound! Cody ignored them. These messages were from a peacetime brain that couldn't understand Cody was fighting for his life.

Deke picked up the heavy steel shovel and crouched for a third assault.

Cody prayed the tiger would strike. Cody *willed* the tiger to strike. Cody focused his thoughts like a laser and *ordered* the huge beast to strike.

In one short leap, Brutus was on Deke's back.

Deke grunted in surprise and sank to the dirt under the weight of the eight-hundred-pound animal.

Brutus took Deke's neck between his teeth.

Even though Deke had been trying to kill him, Cody realized he didn't want the old cowboy dead.

"NO!" Cody shouted, banging his rake against the fence. "NO, BRUTUS, NO!"

Brutus stared at Cody a moment, looking confused.

"LET HIM GO!" shouted Cody, banging the rake. "LET HIM GO *NOW!*"

Brutus released Deke's neck and then backed uncertainly off his prey.

Deke twitched violently and moaned. A puddle of blood spread slowly in the sand.

Swiftly but gently, Cody took Brutus by the collar and led him back into the lockdown area. Then, pulse pounding in his throat and eyes, he raced all the way to the main house, grabbed a phone, dialed 911, and blurted out what had happened.

By the time the ambulance arrived, Deke had lost consciousness.

Twenty-six

"*Well, he's* out of surgery again," said Sunny, making her way carefully into the waiting room of the Saddler's Creek Community Hospital as though she were walking underwater.

"And . . . ?" said Cody.

Sunny sat down beside Cody on the uncomfortable vinyl couch that was the color of rotten avocados and absentmindedly picked up a six-month-old issue of *Newsweek* magazine.

"And he's still alive," said Sunny.

"Well. That's good," said Cody. "I guess."

"But . . . they don't know if he's ever goin' to walk or talk or be much use to anybody again."

Cody thought about this for a while. He noticed there was a jagged rip in the vinyl of the couch. "That's pretty horrible," he said finally.

"Yeah," said Sunny, "it sure is horrible. Well, hon, the man did try to kill you."

"And he tried to frame you for murder," Cody added. "You read that letter from ValCom?"

Sunny nodded. She opened the *Newsweek*.

"Maybe Deke couldn't help it," she said. "No more than Brutus could help leapin' on Deke when he saw his back. Maybe it was just their nature."

Cody shook his head. "Brutus acted without thinking. Deke spent a whole *lot* of time thinking about what he was going to do."

Sunny sighed. "I guess you're right." She turned her attention back to the magazine.

Cody pulled off a small piece of vinyl that looked like it was going to come off the couch anyway.

"Does Deke have any money to pay medical bills?" Cody asked.

"I don't know," she said. "I'll take care of them, though, whatever they are."

"Why? *He tried to frame you for murder,* Sunny."

"I know, hon, but Deke and I go way back. I mean, the man was kind of a daddy to me. A *bad* daddy, but still . . ."

She looked up from the magazine and smiled at him.

"I sure do owe you, darlin'. I surely do. If it wasn't for your comin' up with that signature at the motel . . . and that handwritin' expert swearin' it was Wayland's . . . and the motel clerk swearin' the guy that signed it was the guy in my photos of Wayland . . . I'd now be headed for a big fat murder trial."

"Well, Clive Butterworth would have gotten you off." She snorted with laughter.

"That idiot?" she said. "Deke only hired Clive Butterworth because he's so stupid he would've bungled my case and gotten me convicted. The man couldn't find his butt with a flashlight in both hands."

Twenty-seven

Cody and Sunny were replacing a wall of chain link in a perimeter fence when they heard the voice behind them.

"Once there was a little bunny who wanted to run away," said the voice. "So he said to his mother, 'I am running away.' 'If you run away,' said his mother, 'I will run after you. For you are *my* little bunny.'"

The color drained completely out of Cody's face.

"How do you do, Ms. Carter," said the woman. "I am Dr. Christine Redman."

The woman was attractive, tanned, black-haired, in her mid-to-late forties. Well tailored in an expensive peach-colored suit.

"Dr. Redman, the shrink who's always on the TV?" Sunny asked, impressed.

The woman smiled, showing many teeth. Her fingernails were long, curved, and clawlike. Not red but colorless. *Like a tiger's claws,* Cody thought.

"This boy is my son," said the woman. "I've come to take him home with me. Good morning, Teddy. You've led me on a merry chase, little bunny, but now I've found you at last and I'm taking you back to our hutch."

"I'm not leaving," said Cody in a shaky voice.

"Excuse me?" said his mother.

"You don't even want me back. You only want me back because it's too embarrassing to have a runaway son if you're a famous child psychologist."

"My, my. What a silly thing to say," she said lightly. "Teddy, get your things, dear, and come with me. Hurry now. Chop-chop."

"I'm not ready to go now," said Cody.

"Come on, dear," she said, smiling brightly. "I have the whole day planned. There's a water park about fifty miles back in the direction of the Dallas/Fort Worth airport. If we hurry, we can do the water park, grab a Happy Meal at Mickey D's, and get to DFW in plenty of time for our plane. Sound like fun?"

Cody's mother in her tailored peach-colored suit

seemed an unlikely candidate for Mickey D's, much less a water park.

"I told you I'm not going," Cody said.

Cody's mother glanced at her watch.

"Okay," she said pleasantly. "I can wait a little while till you get your things together. Tell me how much time you need."

"Ten years," said Cody.

His mother's tone changed abruptly.

"All right, Teddy, let's just cut the crap now, shall we? Get your things *immediately* and come with me, or you're going to pay for this when we get home, I promise you!"

She grabbed for Cody's wrist.

Sunny interrupted them. "Excuse me, Dr. Redman," she said. "A boy of sixteen, although a minor, has certain rights. I'll request a hearin' before a family court judge this afternoon in Saddler's Creek. The judge will verify what I just said. In certain circumstances, a sixteen-year-old can get legal emancipation from his parents and then live wherever he chooses."

"Did Teddy tell you he's sixteen?" Cody's mother asked.

"Yes."

"He's a liar," she said. "The boy is fourteen."

Sunny turned to Cody. "How old are you, Cody?"

Cody swallowed hard.

"Fourteen," he said. "And a half."

"You told me you were sixteen." Her voice was stripped of all emotion.

"I'm so sorry," said Cody.

Sunny turned to Cody's mother. "Why don't you come back tomorrow, Dr. Redman, and we can discuss this further."

"Why don't you stay out of a situation that doesn't concern you, dear," said Cody's mother.

"Dr. Redman," said Sunny, "I suggest that you leave now and come back tomorrow."

"I am not leaving here without my son."

"Lady," said Sunny in a steely voice, "you are on my private property and you are now trespassin'. Either leave immediately, or I will call the sheriff and have him personally escort you outta here."

Cody's mother glared at Sunny.

"Get out of my way," she growled, and lunged for Cody.

Sunny stepped between them.

Cody's mother slapped Sunny's face hard. It sounded like a hand clap.

Sunny caught Cody's mother's wrist in midair, held it tight as a trapeze bar, and squeezed it till cracking noises could be clearly heard.

Cody's mother cried out in pain.

"I shall inform the authorities about this incident!" she said, rubbing her injured hand. "Do not think I won't!"

"Oh, I surely hope you do, ma'am," said Sunny. "And if you don't, *I* will."

Cody's mother turned to leave. "I'll be back tomorrow morning, Teddy, with the police!" she snapped. "If necessary, I shall take you with me by force!"

Twenty-eight

"So," said Sunny coolly, "you're fourteen. I seem to recall you sayin' you were *sixteen*. Isn't that what you told me? Showed me a gen-u-wine ID card and everythin'."

"I didn't want to lie to you, Sunny, but it was too late to tell you the truth."

"It's *never* too late to tell anybody the truth," said Sunny.

"I'm sorry I lied to you," he said. "But I really wanted this job, and I didn't think you'd hire me if you knew I was fourteen."

"Well, you got *that* right," she said.

"It's just that I've been so desperate to get away

from my mother, I've been lying about my age for months."

She shook her head and snorted. "I swear, that woman makes a *hornet* look cuddly. Well, Cody, you better pack up and get outta here now, before your mother comes back with the cops."

Cody shook his head. "I'm not leaving," he said.

"You may not have a choice."

"I am through running away from her," he said firmly. "I refuse to spend my whole life running away from her. Sooner or later, I've got to take a stand. I think it's got to be now."

"Well," said Sunny, "it don't make *me* no never mind. Just remember what I told you when you first got here. If a tiger messes with you, yell 'No!' and smack it hard on the nose."

Cody spent a sleepless night, trying to think how to stand up to his mother.

Why was it he could stand up to an eight-hundred-pound tiger but he wilted before a hundred-and-twenty-pound mother? What was the equivalent here of smacking a tiger on the nose? It certainly wasn't physical, at least not with armed cops there. So what was left? Was there *any* area in which his mother was vulnerable?

At seven the next morning, Cody and the tiger wranglers were just finishing up their breakfasts when they heard a crunching on gravel outside the main house. Cody's mother and two uniformed state troopers got out of a police patrol car and entered the house.

The troopers wore high, spit-shined brown boots, brown Smokey the Bear hats, and mirrored sunglasses so you couldn't see their eyes. They had large Smith & Wesson revolvers in brown leather holsters on their hips.

Cody's mother pointed to Cody, and the two troopers swaggered up to him. They were both over six and a half feet tall and looked like brothers.

"Theodore Redman," said one in a strong Texas accent, "being as how you are a minor, fourteen years of age, and an infant in the eyes of the laws of the sovereign state of Texas, you will now voluntarily accompany us off these here premises, or else we shall remove you by force."

Cody didn't answer.

"How do you wish to leave, son—voluntarily or by force?"

Cody didn't answer.

The cop pulled Cody's hands behind his back and cuffed them. The tight steel bracelets were painful on his wrists.

Cody took a deep breath and addressed his mother for the first time in a loud, strong voice.

"You can have me taken from this ranch by force," he said, "but I will *never* live with you—now, or at any time in the future."

Cody's mother started to say something, but Cody continued in his loud, strong voice.

"I have written a letter," he said. "It gives full details about the times you abused me physically. I have addressed copies of this letter to newspapers in New York, Los Angeles, Chicago, Houston, Dallas, San Francisco, and Boston. I gave all the copies of this letter to a friend of mine here at the ranch. If I have to leave here against my will, the letters will go right into the mail the moment I'm gone."

Cody's mother thought this over.

"You are a child, Teddy," she said, controlling her voice. "They will never believe a child."

"I am not a child," said Cody carefully. "I am fourteen years old. I have described all of your abuse in great detail. I have included dates and locations. It is very complete. I know how important your career is to you. I don't think people will have much respect for a famous child psychologist who physically abuses her own son."

"I'll say you made it all up," said Cody's mother confidently. "I'm a nationally known and respected authority. They will *never* take your word over mine."

"Maybe they won't," said Cody. "And then again, maybe they will. Are you really willing to take that big a chance?"

Cody's mother thought about that one for almost a minute.

"Contrary to what you may think," she said in a different tone altogether, "I have been an excellent mother, Teddy. I have given you love. I have given you structure. I have given you boundaries. *Boundaries,* Teddy. Boundaries are a far more important expression of love than hugs or kisses."

She was speaking softly now, as though there were no policemen in the room, no tiger wranglers, nobody but a mother and her son.

"Could I have been more lenient with you?" she asked. "Of *course* I could have been more lenient with you. Absolutely. No question. No doubt about it. And it would have been far easier to do that, I assure you. To let you do whatever you wanted. To let you run wild. You would have *loved* me then, instead of hating me the way you do now. And you would have suffered for it, Teddy, I promise you. You would have suffered for it."

Cody said nothing. Nobody said anything.

"I have been a wonderful mother to you, Teddy. A wonderful mother," she said gently. "You will never *know* how wonderful. You will never know what I had to give up to do it, either, what sacrifices I have had to make. You will never know how much I have loved you. I have been the best mother in the world to you, Teddy. The very best."

She reached into her purse, pulled out a tissue, and dabbed at her eyes. She put the tissue back and closed the purse with an audible snap.

"Release him," she said.

The cops looked at Cody's mother uncertainly.

"I said *release* him!" she snarled.

The cops uncuffed him. Cody rubbed his wrists.

"Goodbye for now, Teddy," said his mother. "Do not think you've seen the last of me. Do not ever kid yourself about that."

Twenty-nine

When the cops and Cody's mother left, everyone congratulated him. He felt great. He felt as if his chest had expanded about a foot. It was like the triumphs with Brutus, only better.

"Well, you sure smacked *that* tiger on the nose," said Sunny.

"What a witch," said Harlan.

"She's meaner than a cold snake," said Randy.

Cody went and poured himself a cup of coffee, his first ever. He didn't much care for the taste. He drank it without either cream or sugar and without waiting for it to cool down. He burned his tongue, but he didn't let on.

"So, Cody," Sunny asked, "what are your plans now?"

Cody took a deep breath and slowly let it out.

"Well, Sunny, I'd really like to stay on here at the ranch," he said.

Sunny nodded seriously.

"You've become a fine tiger wrangler, hon," she said. "A real fine tiger wrangler. What with Deke, Dwayne, and Wayland gone, I'm real short of tiger wranglers. I *would* like you to stay, Cody. But on one condition."

"What's that?"

"Come September, darlin', you enroll yourself at the high school in Saddler's Creek," she said. "Deal?"

He gave her an exaggerated sigh.

"Whatever," he said.

They shook hands.

"By the way," she said, "did you really write all those letters to all those newspapers and leave 'em with somebody here at the ranch to mail, like you told your mom?"

"Aww, Sunny," said Cody "When would I have had the time to do all *that*?"

Six months after Cody became a permanent tiger wrangler at the Sam Houston Tiger Ranch, Detective Runyon drove up from Dallas with news about Sunny's brother.

Wayland had joined the Ringling Brothers circus as a lion tamer when it stopped in Plano. One day during rehearsal, he was drinking more than usual, and he reportedly pushed a cranky old lion a little too hard. The closest emergency room was a good twenty minutes away—without traffic. That day there happened to be traffic. Wayland bled out before the circus truck got even halfway to the hospital.

When she heard about Wayland's death, Sunny locked herself in her bedroom and cried for an hour. Then she never mentioned his name again.

When Cody thought about it, neither Dwayne nor Deke nor Wayland had treated the big cats with the respect that they deserved, and the animals had gotten even. Life doesn't always work out the way you want it to, but sometimes the bad guys get what they deserve.

Author's Note

You may have read this book and found some of the things Cody did with tigers and lions hard to believe. I want to tell you that most of the interactions Cody had with the big cats in *Claws* actually happened to me.

In April 2001, I spent some time at an amazing ranch in Texas that housed sixty-six tigers, half a dozen lions, and assorted leopards and cougars. Like Cody, I got to be good friends with a young male lion who was refusing to eat, and I helped persuade him to call off his hunger strike.

Like Cody, one day I walked into an outdoor pen with four frightening two-hundred-pound Bengal tigers after being warned that they were quite capable of killing me, that they would certainly try to dominate me, and that when they did, I had to yell "No!" and smack them hard on the nose in order to win their respect.

Although gazing at their massive orange and black bodies, their predator's eyes, and finger-length fangs made me weak with fear, I didn't let it show. And when they tried to dominate me, like Cody, I somehow found the courage to smack them hard on their broad, moist noses, and I won their respect.

Over the next several days, I returned to their cages repeatedly, leashed them up, and took them out for hour-long walks around the ranch every morning and every evening, as though they were cocker spaniels and not dangerous jungle beasts. Like Cody, I shoveled their poop, sometimes even when they weren't confined to their lockdown areas, and I hauled rotting, maggot-infested cattle carcasses out of their pens with my bare hands, days after the tigers had begun chowing down on them.

Once, my young lion buddy, who was friendlier than most pups I've met, playfully bit me on the shoulder. I was wearing a leather flight jacket at the time, and you can still see the holes where his teeth went through it.

Another time, a month-old tiger cub irritably bit me on the neck because she was tired of being held after I'd nursed her from a baby bottle and burped her. Her tiny teeth left a pattern of red marks around my Adam's apple but didn't draw blood. I was told our baby girl was merely learning how to kill.

And on one frightening day, because I'd grown careless in a pen containing five older animals and forgot the rule of keeping all five of them in view at all times, a four-hundred-pound tiger crept behind me, reared up on its hind legs, and plunked his enormous paws down on my shoulders. If I'd stopped to think what I was doing, I might not have had the guts to spin around, smack him on the nose, and get him off my back before he really hurt me.

Why would I want to do such dangerous things?

Part of the reason is that I've always admired tigers and I wanted to get to know them intimately. Part of the reason is that when I was a kid growing up in Chicago, my parents were so protective of me, so worried something bad might happen to me, that they made me afraid of almost everything. To overcome my fears, I've spent most of my adult life deliberately seeking out risky things to do.

I found I enjoyed writing about these experiences and that testing myself in risky situations was almost as exhilarating as the writing itself.

—Dan Greenburg

DATE DUE

APR 0 8 '08	DEC 2 1 '09	
OCT 1 7 '08	APR 1 9 '10	
DEC 0 9 '08	APR 1 9 '10	
JAN 0 5 '08	APR 2 9 '10	
APR 0 3 '09	OCT 2 0 '10	
APR 2 9 '09	OCT 2 8 '10	
MAY 1 5 '09	JAN 0 3 '11	
SEP 2 4 '09	APR 2 6 '11	
NOV 0 5 '09		
NOV 1 6 '09		
DEC 0 7 '09		